The Peach Cobbler Caper

A Paranormal Cozy Mystery Novella

B I Skinner

Contents

1. Chapter 1   1

2. Chapter 2   8

3. Chapter 3   16

4. Chapter 4   22

5. Chapter 5   29

6. Chapter 6   36

7. Chapter 7   43

8. Chapter 8   49

9. Chapter 9   54

10. Chapter 10   59

11. Chapter 11   65

12. Chapter 12   72

13. Chapter 13   81

14. Chapter 14   90

15. Chapter 15   101

16. Chapter 16   110

17. Chapter 17   118

18. Chapter 18   126

19. Chapter 19   135

20. Peach Cobbler Recipe   138

More Books by B I Skinner   140

Copyright   142

Chapter 1

"Are we there yet?" Mystery, the talking ghost cat, asks from the backseat of my absurdly bright pink, fully restored, vintage Volkswagen Bus.

"You asked me that five minutes ago," I remind her with a grimace. "Palisade is only an hour away; it's not that long of a drive."

"I've never been on a car ride this long," Clara, my 143-year-old, pink flannel nightgown-wearing roommate, tells us. "At least not as a ghost."

For reasons unbeknownst to the living, most ghosts are tethered to the property where they passed. But, unlike most spirits, Clara and Mystery can ride in our Volkswagen bus, (although they can't leave it). I think it's because the previous owners restored the bus on the property. But it's only a guess on my part.

Recently, I tried giving a ride to a ghost who died in the Glenwood Sport Gym. But the moment I drove off the property, he promptly disappeared from the passenger seat and reappeared on the gym steps. So, it's definitely only Clara and Mystery who can ride along.

"Is Mystery still asking if we're there yet?" Wendy, one of my best friends, and a witch, laughs knowingly. I'm secretly jealous of her vibrant personality and unique appearance. Between her spiky pink hair and the book themed tattoos that adorn her arms, in addition to all her piercings, she is a standout figure in any crowd. Every day, rain or shine, she hops on her mint green Vespa and drives to The Looking Glass, her bookshop at 6th and Maple. She also recently adopted three, yes I said three, Sphynx cats. She insists she'll crochet sweaters for them this winter. I'm still doubtful she'll convince a cat to wear a sweater.

"Of course," I tell her.

Yes, I'm the only one of us who can see ghosts. I'm what they call a Spirit Communicator, and we're extremely rare. If someone has told you they can talk to ghosts, they're probably lying. That's how rare we are.

"I'm so excited you're finally experiencing the annual Palisade Peach Festival!" Juliet, my other best friend, exclaims. Standing a little short and cherishing her delightful curves, she embodies the essence of what every good baker should be – warm, inviting, and full of love. As the motherly figure of our circle, she is our nurturing presence. She's the one we turn to for advice, support, and a listening ear.

She's also the one who will tell me to get over myself which, even though it annoys me, she's right.

The festival started nearly 60 years ago in Palisade, Colorado, where they have the best peaches in the world. They tell me it's due to hot summer days and cool nights, creating the ideal growing conditions for jumbo-sized, sweet peaches with succulent juice that drips down your chin.

The yearly festival features all things peach. Peach eating contests, peach recipe contests, delicious food, dancing, festivities, parades, and even a Peach Queen! I've been looking forward to it for weeks. I'm especially eager to try some wines the local wineries produce in Palisade.

Wendy, Juliet, and I each have a room at the Peach Blossom Inn and Retreat for the weekend, while Mystery and Clara will stay in the VW, of course.

"Are we there yet?" Mystery asks again, licking a paw to groom the long, gray hair on her head. We're not sure how old she is. She claims she forgot. She also insists she could always talk, so she isn't sure why we make such a fuss about it.

"Yes! The next exit is #42, which is Palisade," I explain with as much patience as I can muster.

"Yay!" Mystery and Clara cheer.

As we drive through Palisade's tiny, picturesque town, we admire the tree-lined streets, quaint shops, and vibrant community spirit. And just like they do in Glenwood Springs, young and old alike stop to admire my vivid bus with the lavender daisy painted on the side. We return everyone's waves and honk the horn. Wouldn't they be surprised to learn there are two ghosts inside the bus waving at them as well?

"I can feel the energy from here!" Juliet exclaims. "Everyone is excited about the festival."

"I smell peaches!" Clara giggles.

"The brochure says Palisade has over a half million peach trees," Wendy informs us.

"I want to know where the wineries are," I add, while carefully maneuvering the bus into a parking spot in front of the Peach Blossom Inn. "You promised me wineries!"

We pause for a moment, watching the townspeople bustle about, decorating the streets with peach-themed banners, setting up the stage for lively musical performances, and preparing the starting point for the 5K Peach Run, ensuring every detail is perfect for the upcoming celebration.

My friends talked me into a mini vacation after all the drama we recently experienced with a troublesome ghost who was haunting the Glenwood Sport Gym. Of course, Clara and Mystery insisted they had to come along.

"Welcome! Welcome!" a plump woman with wild curls of silver hair and an infectious smile greets us the moment we step foot in the inn. "I'm Agnes Plumfield, and I'm delighted you're staying with us!" Her fashion sense is as vibrant as her personality. Her striped purple shirt doesn't quite match her floral-patterned magenta skirt, but it works for her. She's added colorful accessories, along with peach-shaped earrings to complete the look.

She loops one arm through mine and one through Juliet's while leading us to the check-in desk, regaling us with stories of past festivals. "At the Peach Blossom Inn, you're not just a guest; you're a cherished member of our family. I take it the drive from Glenwood Springs was pleasant?"

"How did you know we're from Glenwood?" Juliet inquires.

"Oh my dear, I know everything." She smiles so broadly at us I'm instantly at ease. "And you," she looks at Wendy, "I expect one of your world-famous hugs," she insists before bustling behind the counter, leaving us in shock. Everyone in Glenwood knows about Wendy's hugs. But how does Agnes know? I suspect there's more to her than meets the eye.

After we drop off our belongings, in rooms Agnes insists are specifically tailored to our individual needs, Juliet suggests we wander through town to check out the sights.

"This is the cutest town ever," Wendy says.

"So much history," I add.

"Have you seen any ghosts since we arrived?" Juliet asks.

"Two, but I don't think they were interested in talking. I wonder what they have stories to tell."

"Let's stop in here," Juliet says, staring up at the weather worn wooden sign for the Dough & Tell Bakery.

"Of course, we have to check out the bakery," Wendy exclaims with a playful smirk.

"I'm just curious!" Juliet retorts. Juliet is a sun witch and owns the Sol Conceptions Bakery on Grand Avenue in Glenwood. Her bakery is also the reason I have to swim laps in the town hot springs pool every night or I'll blow up into a caricature of the Stay Puff Marshmallow giant.

My gaze locked on the tantalizing pastries showcased in the bakery display, I deliberate over my choices. Should I get a slice of peach pound cake or try a piece of something called opera cake with layers of mouth watering chocolate and espresso buttercream?

The pound cake. Definitely the pound cake. But as I open my mouth to tell the man who is waiting on us I'll have a slice of cake, a piercing scream from the back room shatters the tranquility of the moment.

"What on earth?" Juliet exclaims.

We jump when a woman bolts into the dining area. "It's gone! It's gone!" she cries.

"What's gone?" the man who was helping us asks.

"My award-winning peach cobbler recipe!"

"Are you sure you didn't misplace it? Should you check again?"

"Of course not! I always keep it in the safe," she says, swatting at his head like it's the most ridiculous thing she's ever heard.

"You don't have it memorized?" Juliet asks.

"Yes, I have it memorized, but that's not the point. Someone has stolen a top secret recipe that's been in my family for generations. The Dough & Tell is ruined!"

Chapter 2

Wendy turns to stare at me in surprise, her mouth agape, her eyes wide.

Don't think about it! I transmit to her using my psychic powers. Just kidding. I'm not the least bit psychic. Wouldn't it be useful though? But, I don't have to be psychic to know what she's thinking. And she can forget it. We're here for vacation. We're not here to solve a mystery.

I shake my head at her. "I'm sure the local police are more than capable of handling a burglary by themselves," I tell her through clenched teeth.

If only Sheriff Mack could hear me say that! I drive him crazy with my endless interference in Glenwood crime. I am a licensed paranormal private investigator, after all. People hire me to help solve mysteries.

Sometimes it's as simple as a lost wedding ring (the house ghost told me the cat pushed it off the dresser and into the heating vent), but sometimes it's as complicated as working with a ghost to determine whether he was murdered and, more importantly, who did it. But, as I said, we're here for vacation!

"Oh. I'm sorry. I didn't realize we had customers," the middle-aged woman says through her tears when she realizes we're waiting to order. She pats at her graying hair tied neatly in a bun as if she's trying to compose herself in front of us.

"It's okay, really, we'll be going now," I assure her. If I don't hurry Wendy and Juliet out of here right this minute, this vacation will turn into a work trip.

When the woman's composure cracks, tears devolve into hysterics and hiccuping. Juliet, always the mother figure among us, takes charge. "Ma'am, why don't you sit down so you can tell us what happened?"

The sturdily built man rakes his hand through already tousled salt and pepper hair, and sighs. He looks completely lost until Juliet asks him for a glass of water and tissues which he hurriedly moves to get.

"I'm Juliet, this is Wendy, and this is Holly. We're here from Glenwood Springs for the festival."

"Have I met you before, dear?" the woman blinks up at me through blurry eyes.

"I don't think so," I mutter, staring at the floor. My investigations earned me some publicity, but I doubt it reached Palisade.

"I'm so sorry to be blubbering like this, but I can't believe my recipe is gone."

"It's okay," Wendy insists, patting her back. "What's your name?"

"I'm Evelyn Whitman, and that's my husband, Harold. We've owned the bakery for 30 years."

"Partners in life and business." Harold smiles fondly as he hands her the water and tissues.

Juliet grins back at them. "My name is etched into every corner and crevice of my bakery in Glenwood Springs. I completely understand how it takes not only your heart and soul, but blood, sweat and tears too."

"So, you do understand! Bless you!" Evelyn cries.

"Can you tell us exactly what happened?" I ask as gently as possible.

"I didn't have time to go to the bank yesterday, after we closed," Evelyn continues to hiccup, "so I put all the checks and some cash into the safe. I opened it just now, and it was gone!" she wails.

"They stole your money?" Wendy gasps.

"No, they left the money. They only took my recipe, which I keep in a special box."

"Did anyone else know that's where you keep the recipe?" I ask.

"No, only me and Harold."

"Does anyone else have the combination?" I continue to press. We've gone this far, I might as well keep at it.

"No," she shakes her head sorrowfully.

"How badly was the safe damaged?" I ask. I know, I know, but I can't help myself. It comes naturally these days.

"It wasn't damaged at all."

"So, only you and Harold know the combination of the safe, which was opened but undamaged, and now a recipe no one else knew was in there is gone. Is that correct?" Fizzlesnort candy-coasters, this is getting complicated.

Harold and Evelyn nod.

"Someone else had to have known," I murmur.

"That's what I'm thinking." Wendy nods.

"Now I know why you look so familiar!" Evelyn exclaims.

Uh oh.

"I saw you in the newspaper last winter. You solved the mystery of the missing peridot! You're a ghost whisperer."

"Well, paranormal private investigator, but yes, I talk to ghosts," I nod, my cheeks reddening.

"You're famous here. The entire town was talking about you for weeks. Please! I need you to find the thief who stole my recipe!"

"Well, I, uh, I'm supposed to be on vacation this week-end," I stammer.

"Oh, please! Please help me! I'll pay you anything."

This was supposed to be a relaxing vacation, a chance to unwind from everything that's happened this year. Yet, here I am, being coaxed into solving another mystery.

Evelyn sniffles into her tissue, her eyes red and puffy behind her wire-rimmed glasses. "The recipe is my family's legacy. It's passed down through six generations of Whitman bakers. Without it, I'll lose everything."

"But you said you have it memorized," Juliet reminds her.

"You don't understand; if the thief has it, they can make my peach cobbler. Or they might sell it to some corporate bakery, and mass produce it! Or just post it on the internet for all to see," Evelyn exclaims, wringing her hands.

"My cobbler is legendary. The mere thought of it is enough to bring droves of customers through my door, all salivating in anticipation of its sweet aroma and delectable taste. If everyone else can make it, why would they ever come here again?"

I exchange looks with Juliet and Wendy, who are busy consoling Evelyn's husband, Harold. Of course, they're thinking the same thing. How can we possibly say no?

I squeeze Evelyn's hand and sigh. "Don't worry," I tell her. "We'll get to the bottom of this."

I never had anything from my parents, but if I did and lost it, I would be heartbroken. I was only allowed to take a few things with me into foster care. The rest likely donated to a thrift store or thrown out.

"Alright," I tell her, squeezing her shoulder. "Let's look at the safe. Maybe our thief left behind a clue."

Her eyes light with hope. "Oh, thank you! I feel so much better knowing you're investigating!"

I give her a small smile. If only I was as confident. A recipe, whose location was known only to the Whitmans, is stolen from a safe that only the Whitmans can access? I don't have a clue where to start with this one. It might be all over the internet by now, anyway.

The Whitmans lead us into a small office where, aside from some old filing cabinets and a desk, the room is bare.

"Holly," Juliet whispers, her voice tinged with trepidation.

I tear my gaze away from examining the room, surprised at the seriousness in her tone. "What is it?"

"I can feel it," she murmurs, her eyes darting around the space.

My heart quickens while a shiver runs down my spine. Juliet rarely talks like this. "Feel what?"

"A presence. A dark and deceptive presence," she confesses, her voice still barely above a whisper.

"You mean it's still here? Even now?"

Juliet shakes her head, but her face is still etched with concern. "Not entirely, but the energy in the room is one of deception."

"Someone is lying?" I ask, confused. Deception could mean so many things." "Do you think the theft is paranormal?"

Her eyes meet mine, filled with uncertainty. "It's possible. We can't rule anything out."

"Are we in danger?" Evelyn's voice trembles while Harold pushes her behind him, out of harm's way.

Juliet shakes her head. "There's only traces of it. You're not in danger."

"Let's look at the safe," I insist.

The steel safe is open, but as Evelyn said, there's no sign of damage.

"What's this?" I ponder out loud, kneeling down. "It looks like a tiny flower."

"It's a peach blossom," Evelyn says. "Why would a peach blossom be on the floor near the safe?"

"Because the town is full of peaches?" I respond. That's kind of a weird question, isn't it?

"Peach trees blossom in April and May. Any blossoms would be long gone by now," Evelyn explains patiently.

But as I reach for it, Wendy bats my hand away. "You don't want to touch anything that might be cursed."

"Okay, well, do your thing," I tell her.

Wendy takes a deep breath, allowing the energy of the room to flow through her while holding her fingertips mere inches above the blossom. The air crackles with anticipation while she wields her magic. Stillness settles in the room, like time holding its breath, awaiting her judgment.

"This is no ordinary peach blossom," Wendy informs us. "It's enchanted."

Chapter 3

We leave the bakery with the enchanted peach blossom safely stashed in a delicate handkerchief in Wendy's pocket. (She assured us it's enchanted, not cursed.)

The Whitmans promised to call the police right away to file a report. I don't need another grumpy sheriff on my back, accusing me of interfering in an investigation. *Leave it to the professionals*, Sheriff Mack likes to nag me.

Clara and Mystery will be surprised to learn we're not only here for vacation, but now we have a mystery to solve.

"Uh oh," Mystery says the moment I open the VW door.

"What, uh oh?" I ask.

"You landed another client," she responds with a bored roll of her green eyes.

"How did you--"

"Oh, absolutely they did, my dear Mystery!" Clara agrees enthusiastically.

So much for being surprised. "How can you tell?" I continue to ask.

"You've got the look," Clara insists.

"What look?" Have I mentioned my spirit roommates can be exasperating?

Mystery yawns, stretching out in a patch of sunlight in the backseat. "The look you get when you're on the trail of another criminal. It's pretty obvious."

"Fine. You're right," I sigh.

"Where was the body?" she asks.

"There's no body. An award-winning peach cobbler recipe was stolen from the Dough & Tell Bakery. We also found an enchanted peach blossom on the floor by the safe."

"Peach blossom?" Clara says. "You shouldn't see peach blossoms this time of year."

"That's what Evelyn, the bakery owner, told us."

"What are they saying?" Wendy asks. "You always neglect to catch us up."

"Oh, yeah, sorry. Clara is confirming we shouldn't see peach blossoms this time of year."

"It's enchanted," Wendy says, holding it out opposite to where Clara is sitting.

"She's over there." I point.

"Oh, sorry, here," Wendy says.

"It looks like an ordinary peach blossom to me."

"Wendy insists it's enchanted."

"Do you have any suspects?" Clara asks.

"Evelyn gave us a list of people who have regular access to the back office in the bakery. The first guy we need to talk to is Marcus Reynolds, a produce delivery driver for a company called Freshest Harvest Express. He delivers produce to the bakery bright and early every morning. Sometimes he arrives before they do, so he has a key to let himself in the back. Evelyn insists he'd never steal from them, but Harold says he's shifty. Besides, he missed his regularly scheduled delivery this morning, so we need to find out where he was when the recipe went missing."

"Like that truck?" Clara points to one in front of the coffee shop beside the inn.

"Exactly like that truck! Thanks, Clara!" I point it out to Wendy and Juliet.

"Nice job Clara!" Juliet exclaims while Clara beams.

As we approach the delivery truck, a middle-aged man of average height, but with a slightly hunched posture, as if he's trying to make himself inconspicuous, appears around the corner. His shifty demeanor and cautious eyes hint at someone who likes to keep his distance. He fits Evelyn's description, so I bet it's him.

"Hi, Marcus Reynolds?" I ask, trying to maintain a friendly tone given his guarded disposition.

"Who's askin'?" he grunts in a low, gravelly voice, his narrow-set eyes darting between us.

"I'm here on behalf of Evelyn and Harold Whitman," I reply, hoping the mention of their names might encourage some cooperation.

"Whaaa? Sumthin happen to 'em?" he asks, his voice betraying concern.

"Evelyn's peach cobbler recipe was stolen from the office safe early this morning," I explain, watching for any flicker of reaction.

"Ohhh, dat's bad," he mutters, the lines on his forehead deepening.

"Can you tell us where you were early this morning? She said you missed your delivery," Wendy asks with a practiced non-threatening tone.

"Yeah. Had a mishap at the docking station first thing. You can call my manager and ask," he responds, his voice tinged with a touch of defensiveness. His eyes continue to dart about, never fully meeting our gaze.

"A bunch of crates of produce were damaged, so I had to stay back and help salvage the goods," he insists, as if anticipating our suspicions. His explanation seems plausible, but something about his evasiveness raises my curiosity.

"You can even call my manager and ask," he adds. "Here's a card with the number." He hands me a wrinkled card from his shirt pocket. "Just ask for Frank. You ladies cops or sumthin? Cuz the last thing I need is trouble."

"We're just friends of the Whitmans," Juliet insists.

"They're nice people. Especially Evelyn. Maybe not so much her old man, but she's a nice lady. Say, do you need anything else? Cuz I gotta get back to work. I'm late for everybody's route today on account of da mishap, you know."

"I think we're good for now. Sorry to have taken up your time," I tell him.

"That guy was sweating like a sinner in church," Juliet insists as we walk away from the truck, and I sense the weight of his gaze boring into our backs.

Wendy and I snicker at her southern expression.

"When Juliet gets riled up, y'all better brace yourselves 'cause that East Texas accent of hers ain't just a gentle whisper anymore—it's like a tornado of twang, ready to knock you off your boots and send you flying!" Wendy declares with the worse southern accent I've ever heard.

"Excuse me?" Juliet says, stopping in her tracks while I laugh so hard my sides hurt.

"I couldn't help it. It had to come out," Wendy claims.

Juliet warned me when I first met her that the Texan in her may appear without warning. Especially, like Wendy said, when she's riled up.

"I don't see him having access to an enchanted peach blossom, though," Wendy says, ignoring the stink eye Juliet is still sending her way.

"Good point," I tell her. "Let's head back to the inn before looking for our next suspect. I need to grab some sunscreen and change into more comfortable shoes."

"I wonder what Sheriff Mack would say if he knew we were involved in another mystery," Juliet ponders with a gleam in her eye.

"I knew it was only a matter of time before you brought him up!" I exclaim while they dissolve into a sniggering fit.

"Protest much?" Wendy asks.

Chapter 4

Agnes rushes to greet us the moment we return to the inn. "Darlings!" she exclaims. "You've had quite the introduction to Palisade, haven't you!"

"How did you know?" Juliet asks as we turn to each other in wonderment.

"Everyone knows." Agnes nods, her elaborate peach earrings swinging enthusiastically. "It's all over town. But I'm relieved you're the ones investigating the theft."

"I'm not sure how successful we'll be at finding the recipe, but we'll give it our best shot," I tell her. I hate getting everyone's hopes up. The fact that no one else was supposed to know where the recipe was kept or how to access the safe makes solving this extra tough.

"My dear," Agnes says, clutching my arms, "you must understand it's more than a recipe to the Whitmans. It's not merely a collection of ingredients and measurements. It's an integral part of Evelyn's childhood. A time when she stood alongside her mother, learning the secrets of the orchard and the art of baking. Each scoop of sugar, and each slice of perfectly ripe peach, carry within it a memory of laughter, and warm summer evenings spent gathered around the table, savoring the fruits of their labor. That's what it's about."

Why did she have to put it like that? It was already a difficult case. Now I feel the weight of generations of peach cobbler bakers on my shoulders.

However, when Wendy tries to show her the enchanted peach blossom, we're surprised by what seems like a dismissal. "That's lovely dear, now scoot. You don't want to miss the ice cream social," she insists.

"I don't think we have time for ice cream at the mo--" I try to tell her.

"Nonsense! You girls are here for some downtime. I promise you'll be sorely disappointed if you miss the social."

"But--" She just said she was relieved we're investigating the case, but now she wants us to eat ice cream?

"No buts! It's in Riverbend Park. Go straight out this door, make a right, then make another right, and you're there. You can't miss it. Go!" she insists, pushing us out the door.

"I know we have a mystery to solve, but I've never been one to turn down ice cream, and I'm certainly not starting now," Wendy says.

"All right, fine, we'll get ice cream," I relent as we traipse back out into the bright summer day with Agnes pushing at our backs.

As we approach the park, even I begin to think Agnes is right. This looks like fun. It can't hurt to take a quick break, right? The park is adorned with colorful banners and decorations celebrating the summer spirit and the peaches' arrival. When the scent of freshly baked waffle cones and the sweet aroma of ripe peaches wafts through the air, my stomach reminds me I never got my pastry at the bakery.

A large crowd of ice cream lovers gather around numerous booths showcasing an array of creative flavors, each vying for attention. Enthusiastic vendors, donning cheerful aprons and broad smiles, eagerly scoop generous portions of ice cream into bowls and cones, expertly garnishing each with delectable toppings.

"I'm so glad Agnes talked us into this," Wendy mumbles, staring at the array before us.

"Me too," Juliet whispers back.

We stand, unmoving, unsure which to try first. "Didn't some scientist say if you put a girl between two ice cream flavors, she would become overwhelmed, trying to decide which one to try first, and starve?" Wendy asks.

"Yes, I'm sure the experiment involved ice cream," I tell her.

"She's not wrong, though; how will we ever decide?" Juliet moans.

There's more flavors here than I can count, each with a cleverer name than the last. We have Peachy Swirls 'n Cream in one corner, Peachy Creamy Cheesecake Bliss next to that, and across the way is Bourbon Peach Delight, which, when Juliet sees the banner, she dashes forward to sample. Who knew you could invent so many flavors of peach ice cream? I ultimately choose Peachy Perfection Sorbet.

I eventually find Wendy at a booth several feet away, devouring a grilled peach with a scoop of vanilla ice cream and a sprinkle of saigon cinnamon, nestled in an edible bowl.

"Hey! Where did you get that?" Juliet exclaims, catching up to us again, pulling on the bowl.

"If you take my ice cream, I swear I'll hex you," Wendy growls.

"Is that lady waving at us?" I ask, pointing to a booth nearby.

Standing behind a booth adorned with peach-themed decorations and a banner that reads Peachy Desires, a mysterious woman with flowing auburn hair and an enigmatic smile beckons us.

"Welcome to Palisade, girls. I trust you're enjoying the ice cream?" she giggles softly, while Wendy grins sheepishly, a smear of ice cream on her cheek, a bowl in one hand, a slowly melting cone in the other.

"Come, don't be shy. I'm Genevieve Hawthorne; I own one of the local orchards. You're not from around here, are you?" she says with a voice so serene and melodic we can't help but stare at her, mesmerized.

"That's an intriguing broach," Wendy says, nodding at the pin attached to the filmy scarf draped over her shoulders. It looks exactly like the peach blossom we found in the bakery. Do all peach blossoms look alike? I'm unsure, but there's something about this one.

Genevieve's warm smile widens as she gracefully touches the broach. "Ah, you have an eye for detail, my dear. It represents the essence of an enchanted peach blossom, a symbol of magic and hidden secrets."

"We came across an enchanted peach blossom earlier today. Would you know anything about it? Considering this is hardly the time of year for peach blossoms," I ask.

Genevieve's expression remains serene, yet a flicker of intrigue dances in her eyes. "You're aware of the stolen recipe," she says, thoughtfully.

How on earth would she know a peach blossom is tied to the recipe theft? Unless she's the thief.

"No, my dear, I'm not the thief," she insists, laughing when she notices my stricken expression. "Don't worry. I'm not a mind reader either. The look on your face says it all."

"You obviously know the Whitmans," Juliet points out.

"In a tiny town like this, there's no one I don't know."

"Do you happen to know who stole the recipe?" I laugh nervously, not really expecting an answer. Naturally, I wish it were that easy. Who knows, perhaps one day I'll stumble across a case that is, but for now, I'll work this case like I've done all the others.

"I'm afraid the answer to that question is not so simple," Genevieve says, her voice carrying a mysterious air. She pauses while we lean in. Why must she allow the suspense to linger so? I'm impatient to solve this!

"I fear the answer to who stole the recipe is tangled in a web of secrets and hidden motives. It's a tale that goes deeper than you could imagine. Let's say there are forces at play in this town, forces that crave more than just a taste of victory."

"Forgive me for being so obvious, but what do we do with the blossom?" I ask. All this mysterious talk is frustrating me. Why doesn't she just give us the answer?

"The enchanted peach blossom is not merely a small flower; it holds a connection to the ancient magic that surrounds us. When you and your friends need guidance, its light will shine brighter, illuminating the path you must take."

"You mean it will literally light up or figuratively?" I press. She must think I'm the most annoying person ever.

"Listen to your intuition. The enchanted peach blossom chose you and your friends as its bearer for a reason. Trust in that."

I exchange glances with Wendy and Juliet. This innocent journey for a missing recipe has suddenly become a tantalizing quest filled with magic and intrigue. How were we to know, when we decided to come here, that Palisade held secrets far beyond its picturesque orchards?

Chapter 5

"Didn't Evelyn tell us Lillian Hawthorne is a rival baker and a potential suspect?" Juliet says as we reluctantly walk away from Genevieve's booth. I don't know what it is about her, but we struggled to tear ourselves away from her charismatic aura. We were battling between the desire to discover more about the magic and intrigue swirling around her and the pressing urgency of our investigation.

"She did," I respond, following her gesture to a sign proclaiming *Lillian's Delights*. "That must be her!" I exclaim, staring at the woman in her late 40s with shoulder-length chestnut hair who's regarding the crowd with an intense gaze. "She fits Evelyn's description."

"Let's check it out," Wendy says.

"Good afternoon, ladies," Lillian greets us with a guarded smile. Is she suspicious of us already? "Can I interest you in a sample of my peach cobbler? It's my specialty."

"Yes, please!" Wendy says, her hand outstretched, as if she didn't just eat her weight in ice cream. Wendy can eat almost anything, and it never shows, unlike Juliet and me, who put on weight from merely smelling pastries. I'm sure it's true. Nothing else explains it.

Lillian expertly uses her pie server, placing a small piece on each plate, which we then eagerly dig into. It's good. I mean, it's really good. I haven't had the chance to try Evelyn's yet, but if it's better than this, I understand why Lillian would be resentful. She creates something this good, only to lose the contest year after year to someone who's even better?

It's so good I'm unsure why she'd want to steal a recipe. She undoubtedly gets a ton of customers as it is. Perhaps she stole it out of spite to sell to the highest bidder or post on the internet?

She wouldn't win any trophies, but if she's as bitter as Evelyn claims, she may do it purely out of spite. Didn't Genevieve tell us the theft is about forces craving more than victory? Their rivalry might be less about a trophy and more about revenge.

"This is amazing," Wendy says, her mouth full of cobbler.

"Thank you. I've worked hard to get where I am. Unlike some people, who were handed an award-winning recipe,"

Lillian says, glaring at the Dough & Tell booth, "some of us have to develop our own."

"Speaking of recipes, we'd like to ask you a few questions," I jump in. It's not like we have unlimited time here.

"Oh?" Lillian's expression turns even more guarded.

"We're investigating the theft of Evelyn's peach cobbler recipe," Juliet says.

"I see," Lillian responds, her eyes narrowing. "And what makes you think I had anything to do with it?"

"We heard about your rivalry with Evelyn. How she wins the peach cobbler contest year after year, and you always come in second."

Lillian grits her teeth. "I'm sure Evelyn told you I'm a sore loser when it comes to the contest. But it doesn't mean I'm willing to steal a recipe. Talent, skill, and a touch of cunning separate the winners from the losers."

I can't help but notice how she proudly lifts her chin at the word cunning. "Cunning as in cheating?" I ask.

"What's that supposed to mean?"

"Evelyn told us about the time you cheated," Wendy says between bites of cobbler.

"The baking competition in Grand Junction?" she snorts. "Of course, she'd bring it up. What did she tell you?"

"We'd like to hear your side of the story."

"I may have tripped and accidentally added a cup of salt to Evelyn's red velvet cake batter when she wasn't looking."

"Accidentally?"

"Whatever. Things happen, you know."

"What about the 10-year-old boy in the audience who saw you *accidentally* add salt to Evelyn's cake? Did he know you tripped before he reported you to the judges?"

Lillian's expression briefly flickers with a combination of guilt and defiance while she leans in closer, her voice dripping with controlled aggression. "I won't deny I've pushed boundaries in the past, but I'm not a thief. I may play dirty sometimes, but I'm not foolish enough to jeopardize everything over stealing some old recipe which isn't that great anyway, if you ask me. I have my pride."

I have to keep pushing here. Even though she claims she didn't steal it, she's obviously angry. "It must be frustrating for you. Losing to Evelyn year after year."

Her smile tightens, eyes gleaming with resentment. "Frustrating doesn't begin to describe it. I've dedicated my life to baking, honing my skills, and perfecting my recipes. Yet, no matter how hard I try, somehow, Evelyn always outshines me. With a recipe, she didn't create herself. Her family created it. It's not fair." She pouts, blowing her bangs from her eyes with a frustrated sigh. "This town doesn't deserve someone of my caliber. Imagine if their precious peaches ceased to exist. Where would they be then? Nowhere! Just a tiny town with nothing to offer," she continues to mutter so quietly I can barely hear her.

"I know you say you didn't steal it, but for the record, can you tell us where you were early this morning?" Juliet asks.

"Of course. I was being interviewed on television for the popular morning talk show, Rise and Shine Palisade. They interview me every year, you know."

"This is a show on television?" Wendy asks while Juliet bites her lip to keep from laughing.

"Yes, it's a show on television," Lillian snaps. "They cover the festival extensively, featuring key players like me, of course, along with local farmers, winemakers, and artisans who are involved with bringing all of this to life," she explains sweeping her hands in front of her. "It's obviously a very big deal to be on the show. Their segments are quite captivating."

"How long was the interview?" Wendy asks before I can get the question in. Unless she was interviewed for hours she would have had time to steal the recipe.

"I know exactly what you're thinking, but there's a lot more involved with being on television than you realize. There was makeup and wardrobe and the pre-interview and all that. So, no, I didn't steal Evelyn's precious recipe. I couldn't. I was too busy being watched by thousands of people when it was stolen."

"Thousands?" Juliet asks as we walk away. "More like dozens I'd wager."

"Don't let her hear you say that!" I warn her.

"I assume it will be easy enough to confirm her alibi by talking to the people at the television station," Wendy grumbles after we had to tear her away from the peach cobbler. "By the way, in case you didn't notice, she's a witch."

"Really?" I ask.

"Yep. I'd say a spell witch but I can't be certain."

"Well we're definitely following up with hers and Marcus' alibi," I insist, looking back at Lillian, who continues to regard us with a mixture of suspicion and disdain. "Especially when Lillian has a clear motive and a history of cheating."

While we continue to wander around the festival, with the sun beating down on us, my skin is starting to burn. I'm about to suggest we take a break for water and fresh sunscreen when I spot something that makes my heart skip a beat.

"Who's the man Evelyn is arguing with?" I ask.

"Beats me," Wendy says. "We aren't from around here, remember?"

"But should we be worried? It looks pretty heated."

"Let's check it out," Juliet says.

But when we approach, the man abruptly turns on his heel and stomps away. Evelyn looks steamed. Is he another suspect?

"Evelyn, are you okay?" Juliet asks.

"Yes, my dears, I'm fine," she sighs.

"Who was that man?"

"No one you need to concern yourselves with. Just old business," she scolds, busying herself with tidying her already neat booth.

I don't care what she claims. It looked an awful lot like current business to me.

Chapter 6

"You gals look like you need more sunscreen," Evelyn warns us, changing the subject abruptly. "Hats would help, too," she scolds when we continue to stare at her openmouthed.

Clearly, she isn't willing to explain what we witnessed. Not at the moment, anyway. "She's right," I relent. "I think I've had about all the sun I can take for now. I'd love to go back to the inn and relax. Maybe even dig into the book I brought with me."

"Didn't Agnes say she serves tea at 2:00?" Wendy asks.

"I could go for some tea," Juliet says.

"Don't forget the cookies!" Wendy laughs, rubbing her belly and sighing.

When I turn back to tell Evelyn we'll catch her later, only the top of her head is visible - her booth now swarming with people begging for peach cobbler and other goodies. "Back to the inn it is. We can talk to Evelyn later," I tell them.

I barely make it a few steps when I hear a noise from behind a nearby tree. "Pssst! You, with them purple eyes. Over here. I know ye can see me," a ghost beckons to me.

"There's a ghost who wants to talk to me. Why don't you head back to the inn, and I'll find out what he wants. I shouldn't be long," I tell them.

"Okay, see you in a bit," Wendy says.

"Hello there. Why are you hiding?" I ask him. "I'm the only one who can see you."

"You be the only human who can see me. The name's Jasper McAlister," he announces, bowing in my direction. He wears tattered, dirt-streaked clothing; his weathered face eternally adorned with a thick, unkempt beard reminiscent of a gold miner in the late 1850s.

"I know other ghosts can see you, silly," I remind him.

"Tis' not what I mean," he says, shaking his head.

"Oh! Wait! There are other paranormals here?" I ask, intrigued. I assume he means aside from the two witches I just sent back to the inn.

"Aye, there be otherworldly creatures here, miss."

"Such as?" Obviously, I'm aware of a variety of otherworldly creatures, but what kind would a ghost hide from? And while I don't mean to be rude, I'm not sure I care at this point. I'm tired and parched while a large glass of iced tea in an air-conditioned room is calling to me. I need a polite way to excuse myself from this conversation before I pass out. If only he would walk with me, but he's clinging to the tree like it's a lifeline.

"The Indigo Midnight Shifters be stirrin' in the shadows, miss! Keep a wary eye and an iron grip on yer nerves, for their otherworldly presence treads upon these very grounds!"

Indigo Midnight Shifters? It sounds like a band. Is he pulling my leg?

"Don't tell me ye ain't heard of em!" he exclaims.

"I'm sorry, but I haven't." I shake my head.

"But blast me for a fool, 'tis a blue moon month, I tell ya!" he shouts. It's good that no one else can hear him because he's getting downright belligerent. "A rare occurrence, it is, when the moon turns blue and taints the night sky with its eerie glow. The Indigo Midnight Shifters be restless, mark me words, for the veil between worlds grows thin during such celestial wonders. Do ye even know what a blue moon month be, miss?"

"Yes, I know what a blue moon month is. It's when we experience two full moons in one calendar month," I recite the best I can recall from my astronomy class in high school.

"The last blue moon was two years ago this same month!" he exclaims.

"Oh! Well, what a coincidence," I laugh while he squints at me. I'm still not sure what he's getting at or why it's important. He clearly expects me to take this seriously, but it's kind of difficult. I need to move out of the sun and he's going on about some paranormal being that for all I know lives only in his imagination. "I think I get it now. These Indigo creatures only appear during a month with a blue moon?"

"Aye, that it be, miss. 'Tis as simple as that, no more nor less."

Now we're getting somewhere! "Are these blue men evil?" I ask him. If they're real, should I be worried?

"I reckon they ain't quite evil, but they're beins' that thrive on chaos and mischief, takin' pleasure in stirrin' up trouble 'mongst the paranormal and normal folk alike. They're mischievous critters, unpredictable as a rattlesnake, with a knack for causin' mayhem and spreadin' discord wherever they roam."

"I appreciate the heads up, and I'll be watching for them. But if you don't mind, I'd like to go back to the inn now. It was nice talking to you. Maybe I'll catch you again sometime."

"I've been keepin' an eye on ye all day I have," he steps closer as I try to leave. "Seems like you and yer friends are nosin' 'round, investigatin' the case of the missin' cobbler recipe, am I right?"

"How did you... hold on a second. Did the blue men steal the recipe?" This opens up a whole new world of possibilities! Is this what Genevieve was talking about when she said it was a tale that goes deeper than we can imagine. I'd say this is way deeper than I can imagine.

"How do I find these blue ghosts?" Drat! What did he say they were called again?

"They ain't no ghosts, I tell ya. And ye don't stumble upon 'em, no ma'am. They find ye, they do."

"So, how do they find me? What do they look like? Will I be able to see them if they aren't ghosts?"

"Ye'll know, missy. Ain't no mistakin' it when ye come face to face with 'em. The air gets chill, the hairs on yer neck stand up, and ye feel a presence ye can't quite explain. Ye'll know, mark my words."

"So basically, I stand here and wait for one to come along?" This is so frustrating! He brings me this far, only to tell me I have to wait. I still don't understand what they have to do with the missing recipe, but he's the one who brought it up. They must be connected.

"If ye insist, ye might wanna give the enchanted orchard a go. 'Tis said to hold secrets beyond mortal reckonin', with whispers of ancient magic floatin' through its branches. But tread carefully, for the orchard's enchantments be unpredictable, and ye may find more than ye bargained for."

"Enchanted orchard? Where is this enchanted orchard? Is that where the enchanted blossom came from? " I ask, but he disappears without answering. "Wait! Come back! I'm not done!" I call out, as several people who are walking by pause, concern clouding their faces. "Too much sun! I'll be fine!" I tell them, waving them on.

Why must spirits be so exasperating? Why did he have to leave dangit? I need answers. I stumble back to the inn, my head spinning with everything he told me. Why can't they all be as simple as the poltergeist who flushed a safe deposit key down the toilet?

The cool blast of air conditioning hits me when I walk through the front door. I sigh with relief. Now, where's that iced tea? Perhaps Agnes will make it a long island ice tea because I could use one right now.

I find Wendy and Juliet in the parlor, and of course, Wendy is chewing on a cookie. Where does she put it all?

"Holly, my dear, I'm so glad you're back," Agnes says when she appears from the kitchen with another plate of cookies in her hands. "My stars, you look like you've seen a ghost!"

"I have seen a ghost, and you won't believe what he told me!"

Chapter 7

The moment Jasper's story leaves my lips, Juliet and Wendy's eyes shine with excitement. Juliet springs to her feet, her chair scraping against the wooden floor before tipping over. "An enchanted orchard! Can you imagine?" she exclaims in an uncharacteristically devil-may-care manner for her. What has gotten into this girl? Is Agnes actually serving spiked iced tea? If she is, I'm all in!

"Where is this mysterious orchard?" Wendy asks, who also appears ready to leap from her seat but pauses to finish her cookie. I expect that kind of eagerness from her.

"He didn't say," I explain, taken aback by the giddiness. I was convinced I'd have to search for the enchanted orchard alone. Or at least endure pushback from Juliet. Perhaps it's the witch in them that has them so excited. I think sometimes they secretly wish they, too, could talk to ghosts. If only they knew on some days, I wish I could trade places with *them*.

I turn to ask Agnes if she's heard of such a thing, expecting her to be just as excited, providing us with directions straight to the orchard. I'm surprised to find her wearing a somber expression instead.

She sighs heavily, regarding me with a cautious gaze. "While I understand and appreciate your eagerness to assist my dear friend Evelyn, using any means possible, I fear this enchanted orchard may bring peril and uncertainty."

"So you've heard of this magical place?" Wendy asks.

Agnes pauses as if she's searching for the right words lest she offend us. "Yes, my dear, I have indeed heard whispers of this enchanted orchard," she responds, her voice laced with caution. "I worried that when you showed up with the enchanted blossom, eventually you'd ask about the orchard as well. Legends and tales have circulated throughout Palisade for generations about such a place, each more fabulous than the rest. Although this is the first time I've heard of a ghost relaying the story," she says, nodding at me with a small smile.

"Do you know where we could find it?" Juliet asks.

Agnes is clearly uncomfortable with this conversation. I imagine she doesn't get many visitors like us. We haven't even told her we have two ghosts who came with us!

But I'd like to know more about this orchard. I don't know why an enchanted peach blossom was left in the

Whitman's bakery, but given my conversation with Jasper, I have to believe they're linked.

"While the allure of the orchard may be strong, if it does indeed exist, you must approach it with caution and respect. I fear it's a realm where the lines between reality and fantasy blur, and there could be pitfalls you never encountered before. As for its location, I don't know," she says, placing a gentle hand on my arm. "Trust your instincts, my dear. While the enchanted orchard may hold secrets, it may also be a labyrinth of uncertainty. Assuming you find it, you must be wary of the dangers that lurk within."

After righting her chair, Juliet slumps down at the table, obviously realizing we won't be visiting this enchanted orchard within the next few minutes. Wendy has returned to eating cookies, and I want the iced tea I never got.

"I'm sorry, dear. Where are my manners? You came in here looking for iced tea, and I've been prattling on with cautionary tales."

How does she do that? "I would love a glass of iced tea," I tell her, nodding.

"You have a seat, relax, and I'll be right back with more. Although I'm afraid you'll have to make do with an or-dinary glass of iced tea for now. We don't serve cocktails until dinnertime, but I have a semi-sweet peach wine from a local vineyard I think you'll enjoy."

I'm not even going to ponder how she knows this time. I'll just go with it. And I'm dying to try a peach wine!

"Here you go, dear," Agnes says, placing a tall glass filled to the brim with iced tea on a lacy coaster in front of me. Beads of condensation roll down the slick surface, and if it's possible to drool over a glass of iced tea, I'm doing it. When I grab the glass, the chill rests against my fingers and I sigh with satisfaction. Jasper and the enchanted orchard can wait. As I bring the cool glass against my lips and take that first refreshing sip, a man walks into the inn.

"Good afternoon Mr. Harrison," Agnes says, "we've been expecting you."

It's the man who was arguing with Evelyn in the park!

"Holly, are you okay?" Wendy asks, patting my back as I choke on the iced tea I half spit onto the table. Why is it so hard for me to enjoy some tea today?

"Did you try to swallow too much too soon?" Agnes asks.

"I'm fine!" I wave my hand in the air. "Just swallowed the wrong way," I insist, reluctantly placing the glass on the table.

"Wait, isn't that--" Wendy whispers as I nod furiously.

"Right this way, Mr. Bellamy," Agnes says, placing her hand against the small of his back to guide him to the check-in desk; but not before I find myself locked in a chilling gaze with him. His eyes, a deep and penetrating shade of steel-gray, hold an unsettling intensity, sending shivers down my spine.

"What was that all about?" Wendy whispers after they're out of earshot.

"I'm not sure," I whisper back, "but it's high time we had a second discussion with Evelyn."

"That was really creepy!" Juliet says. "The look he gave you. It's like he knows something."

"Agnes, who is that man?" I ask when he leaves to get his luggage.

"That's Harrison Bellamy," she says. "He's a high-powered executive from a large food corporation, specializing in mass-producing recipes. He's staying in a room on the second floor. Why do you ask?"

"We saw him arguing with Evelyn in the park this afternoon," I explain, my heart racing with anxiety. What if he's after Evelyn's peach cobbler recipe? What if he stole it?

Agnes regards me with a puzzled expression. "Arguing? With Evelyn? Are you sure? Why would he be arguing with Evelyn? Everyone loves her."

"We need to talk to her again. Right now," I insist, standing up from my chair. "She's holding something back, and if she expects us to find her recipe, she'll have to be honest with us."

"You should take an umbrella with you," Evelyn insists, handing us one from a stand next to the door. "It's going to rain."

"Rain? How can it rain? There isn't a cloud in the--" I stop short when Wendy opens the door, the quiet sanctuary of the inn abruptly shattered by a gust of wind sweeping past us.

The once brilliantly sunny day is now choked with dark clouds gathering in the sky, transforming the horizon into a brooding canvas. A powerful wind howls and whistles, forcing trees to sway and leaves to rustle in a frenzied dance.

When we look back at Agnes in shock, she shrugs and smiles. "That's Colorado for you!"

Chapter 8

"Are you sure it's safe to be out in this storm?" Wendy shouts as we huddle under the umbrella, struggling to make our way to Dough & Tell.

"No!" I shout back. "But the sooner we talk to Evelyn, the better. What if Bellamy knows we're on to him? He could be long gone by the time the storm lets up, and it will be too late."

"Did I miss something? How are we on to him?" Juliet also shouts over the wind.

"He has to know something. You saw the way he looked at me back there. Maybe he recognized me like Evelyn did. Either way, I want to find out what's up with him and Evelyn."

The heavy, humid air crackles with electricity as the summer storm takes shape. Swirling, ominous gray clouds cast shadows over the landscape, providing a dramatic backdrop for a confrontation.

Evelyn can deny it all she wants. What I saw between her and Harrison Bellamy was most definitely an argument. And he's a corporate bigwig whose job is selling mass-produced baked goods. They have to be related.

A distant rumble of thunder resonates through the atmosphere, building in intensity with each step we take. The first droplets of rain fall, gentle and sporadic at first, dampening the streets with their touch. Revelers attending the festival run for cover inside their cars and nearby buildings. Merchants rapidly close their booths with a practiced hand. They're obviously used to the dramatically changing Colorado weather, as Agnes pointed out.

We quicken our steps when the rain intensifies, but we're too late. The storm transforms into a steady downpour within seconds. The umbrella hangs from my hand in tatters thanks to the vicious wind, and it occurs to me I don't even know if Evelyn is in the bakery. What if she's still at the festival? What if she's gone home? My insistence we question her immediately may have been a mistake. Why do I have to be so stubborn?

But when I tug on the door, and it opens, I sigh with relief. Evelyn stares at us in disbelief while our soaked clothing creates puddles on her bakery floor. I clutch the mangled remains of the umbrella with a mix of embarrassment and regret. Should I apologize? Make a joke? Jump right in and confront her?

With the door safely closed behind us, the heavens unleash their fury. Rain pounds relentlessly on the roof while booming echoes of thunder shake the store's foundation. The aroma of freshly baked bread mingles with the dampness, creating an odd mixture of the storm's intensity and the comforting scents of dough rising and pastries baking.

"What are you doing here?" Evelyn asks.

"We have questions," I tell her, not feeling quite as confident as I did when we left the inn and didn't look like drowned rats. "Who is Harrison Bellamy to you?"

"I don't know who you're talking about," she claims, her eyes widening momentarily, a flicker of concern crossing her face.

I pause, hoping to use silence against her. People aren't used to silence, so I often find if I wait long enough, they'll talk to fill the void. It's almost an unconscious response. It's something Sheriff Mack taught me. But don't tell Wendy and Juliet I remembered it. They'll just take it the wrong way. She glares at us, but we offer nothing except the sound of our wet clothes dripping water on the floor and the ongoing turmoil of the storm outside.

"I assure you. Harrison Bellamy doesn't have anything to do with my stolen recipe," she interjects, as I predicted she would, but why did she offer the theory that Harrison didn't steal the recipe when I'd said nothing of the sort?

"If you want us to find your recipe, we need your complete honesty," I scold her.

When Evelyn glances around nervously, as if she's afraid someone might overhear, I realize she's keeping secrets. "Is this something you don't want Harold to know about?" I ask gently.

"Can't you come back later?" she begs. "I'm expecting him at any moment."

"I'm sure he ducked in somewhere to avoid the storm. And if you think we're going back out in it, you're mistaken. You might as well tell us while we're here and alone."

"You must promise me you won't repeat what I'm about to tell you. Not to Harold and not to anyone. There's no telling what might happen if he found out."

Juliet steps forward, her flip-flop making a strange squishing noise on the tile floor. "Evelyn, whatever it is, I'm sure--"

"Promise me!" she barks, cutting off Juliet's words of reassurance.

What happened to the sweet little old lady we met earlier today? What has her so distraught?

"Okay, if you don't want us to tell Harold, we won't. I can't imagine what would be so bad," Wendy assures her.

She releases a heavy sigh, burdened by the weight of the world resting on her shoulders. "I'm afraid of how he'd react if he knew. Don't get me wrong, my husband is a gentle and kind man, but if he knew what Harrison was doing to me, there's no telling what he'd do."

"Why?" I ask, my mind awhirl. I can't picture Evelyn doing anything that would make Harold violent. What would Harrison be doing that has her so afraid?

"Harrison Bellamy is blackmailing me," she says.

Chapter 9

"I didn't see that coming," Juliet whispers behind me.

"Blackmail?" Wendy gasps.

"I stole the peach cobbler recipe," Evelyn says. "I stole the recipe," she repeats; the confession falling from her trembling lips, laden with guilt and regret.

My mind struggles to process her confession while Juliet and Wendy stare at her open-mouthed, their eyes wide with disbelief.

"I didn't see that coming either," Wendy whispers.

"You... you stole your own recipe?" I finally piece the words together after a shocked silence.

"Well, not me. And not this morning, if that's what you're thinking!" she exclaims in horror when she realizes how it sounds. "My family stole it. Or at least it's what I'm told."

"This is all very confusing," I admit.

"The story I tell everyone about how I got the recipe isn't entirely accurate," she whispers, wringing her hands with grief.

"You mean the story you tell everyone about the recipe being passed down for six generations?"

"Yes!" she wails.

"Hold on. I'm still confused." I hold up my hand to stop her from continuing. "What do you mean, it isn't entirely accurate? And how is Harrison blackmailing you? Maybe we should sit so you can start at the beginning."

We quickly grab four chairs from a nearby table and settle ourselves down, our expressions a blend of astonishment and confusion. I can't imagine where she's going with this.

"Harrison Bellamy is driven by insatiable ambition. He has pursued me relentlessly for years for my family recipe. He once told me he'd get it using any means necessary. Each time, he offered more and more money, but each time, I refused. It made Harold so mad he threatened to punch him. But then I didn't hear from him for quite some time. I was so sure he'd given up, and you can imagine the relief I felt when I assumed I'd never hear from him again. Then one day, out of the blue, he showed up unannounced. Thankfully, Harold was fishing for the weekend in Gunnison Gorge, or I fear he would have done some-thing drastic."

I know I should ask her a question, but I'm still in shock and can't think of how best to word it. What did Harrison do to this poor woman? Of course, I'm thinking of all sorts of horrible things. I wish she would spit it out already.

"He showed up with a pile of faded pages and dusty archives proving that my ancestors," she almost chokes on the words while stifling a sob, prompting Juliet to leap from her seat in search of tissues, "stole the recipe from a rival baker!"

"So, it hasn't been handed down through generations?" I exclaim, my voice caked with disbelief.

"Oh, it was, but only after my ancestors stole it!"

"You're certain the documents are real?" Wendy asks. "I wouldn't put it past this guy to fake them."

Evelyn nods sorrowfully. "It was my first reaction as well. But I took the documents to an authenticator in Denver, and he confirmed they were real. I tried to track down the descendants of the original baker, but according to the genealogy archives, they died off long ago. The baker only had two daughters, who died from consumption. I'm so ashamed I don't know what to do. Harrison is threatening to tell the world of my family's dark past if I don't sell the recipe to him."

"Oh, Evelyn," I sigh, taking her hand in mine. "You must tell Harold. You shouldn't have to bear this burden alone."

"Even about the blackmail?" she whimpers.

"Especially about the blackmail! In fact, you need to tell the police as well. What Harrison is doing is illegal! What your ancestors did was wrong, but it was a long time ago. And you tried to make it right, but you can't help it if there was no one to give the recipe to."

"If you had known the true story of how your family got this recipe, to begin with, would you have kept up the lie?" Juliet asks gently.

"Oh, my heavens no!" Evelyn exclaims. "I've been telling the story all my life. I hate that it's all a lie, and I never would have continued if I'd known."

"Wow, what a storm!" Harold exclaims, bursting through the front door with such force we all jump as if a thunderclap sounded inside the bakery.

"Oh, I'm sorry, I didn't realize we had compa-- what's wrong?" he asks when he sees the looks on our faces. "Oh no, is it about the recipe? Did you find the thief? They've done something with it, haven't they?"

"We haven't found the recipe, unfortunately, but I assure you, we're still looking. We have to head back to the inn. Agnes is expecting us for dinner, and you two should talk. I promise I'll update you the moment we learn some-thing new," I tell him, eager to leave so Evelyn can talk to Harold.

"Okay, nice to see you again, and thanks for stopping by," Harold tells us.

And just like that, the storm is done. The clouds have given way to sunshine while the town smells just-rained-fresh. There's a pleasant coolness to the air as we walk back to the inn in stunned silence.

Chapter 10

While we make our way back to the inn, a heavy silence settles among us; the weight of Evelyn's revelation lingers while we trudge along the rain-soaked sidewalk. Eventually, Wendy breaks the silence. "I can't believe it," she mutters, shaking her head. "Poor Evelyn. What a burden to carry alone."

I chew on my lower lip, something I haven't done since I was a kid. "I hope she's telling Harold right now."

Wendy's brow wrinkles. "I hope Harold doesn't do something he'll regret!"

"You don't think he'd get violent, do you?" Juliet asks.

"He doesn't seem like the type, but Evelyn was apprehensive. Hey, let's check in with Mystery and Clara before we go inside," I tell them as we approach the inn.

"Thank goodness you're here!" Clara exclaims.

"Why? What's wrong?"

"We overheard those two dudes arguing!" Mystery insists.

"That helps a lot." I roll my eyes. "What two dudes?"

"Dudes? What about dudes?" Wendy pushes me aside as if she can hear Mystery.

"Mystery says they heard two dudes arguing," I tell her, returning the shove.

"One of the men staying at the inn and the man you questioned about the missing recipe earlier," she explains.

"Marcus Reynolds?"

"Yes! That's him."

"Was the other guy Harrison Bellamy?"

"Who's Harrison Bellamy?" Clara asks.

"Let's say we have a lot to catch up on. What did the other guy look like?"

Mystery leans out the window, sniffing at Wendy's hair, which, although Wendy can't see her, still makes her jump a little. "He's tall and grumpy looking. Like Sheriff Mack!"

"I miss the Sheriff," Clara sighs. "He's dreamy."

"We've only been gone for a day!" I remind her.

"Sheriff Mack is better looking than the guy we saw," she points out.

"Great. That also helps a lot." And no, I'm not telling Juliet and Wendy what Clara said, even though she's right.

"He was wearing an expensive suit with polished shoes and stiff hair," she adds.

"Yep, that's Bellamy!"

Wendy drums her fingers on the side of the bus, glaring at me. "Oops, sorry," I tell her. "Clara and Mystery overheard Marcus Reynolds and Harrison Bellamy arguing."

"Just now?" Wendy asks.

"No, before the storm started," Mystery says. "The one dude went into the inn after you did, but then he came out. He was pulling a suitcase from his car when the other dude approached him, and they argued."

"What did they argue about?" I ask.

"I couldn't hear anything because the wind was so loud. But they were definitely fighting."

"Mystery says they argued right after Bellamy checked in. But she couldn't hear them because of the wind," I translate.

"Let's confront Bellamy right now," Wendy insists.

"I'm game," I tell her.

"Let's go, ladies!" Juliet exclaims, surprising me once again with Vacation Juliet.

"You girls wash up. Dinner is almost ready," Agnes says the moment we walk into the inn. This kind of insight no longer surprises me, but I'd love to know her secret. Wendy and Juliet told me they don't sense she's a witch. Is she psychic? Clairvoyant? I wish I knew.

"The storm cooled things off a bit, so I'll serve dinner on the patio this evening," she tells us.

"We have something we need to attend to first, if you don't mind," I start.

"Nonsense. Dinner first. Business later," she insists.

"Is it okay if we ask what's for dinner?" Wendy whispers in my ear.

"We'll start with a grilled romaine salad topped with tomato and Vidalia onions, which a friend of mine brought back from Georgia last week, all tossed with olive oil, vinegar, and a hint of gorgonzola. The main course is a creamy tomato pasta with burrata. The tomatoes are from Sid's farm, of course. And we mustn't forget the loaves of rustic bread from Dough & Tell. The golden-brown crust crackles at the slightest touch. I promise it's heavenly."

When I open my mouth to remind her about the peach wine, she cuts me off. "I didn't forget the wine. It's chilling as we speak if you'd like to pour a glass."

"That sounds amazing, Agnes. I'm famished!" Wendy exclaims.

I can't remember the last time I ate today; meanwhile, Wendy, who hasn't stopped eating, is still famished. I'll never fully understand that girl.

Dinner was epic. I'm not sure I've ever had a meal this good. "Agnes, you've outdone yourself," I tell her.

"Don't forget the dessert," she says as she proudly makes her way onto the patio carrying a breathtaking confection. She tells us she made it with alternating layers of peaches, cream cheese, and whipped topping. Who cares what's in it. It looks fabulous.

"Will we ever tire of these peaches?" Juliet asks.

"No!" Wendy and I exclaim in stereo.

"Is Harrison Bellamy here?" I ask Agnes after she's placed a slice of dessert on our plates.

"I haven't seen him since he checked in," she tells us.

Throughout dinner, I alternated between hoping he'd show up so I could question him, and hoping he wouldn't, because I didn't want to spoil our dinner.

After thanking Agnes profusely for such a delightful meal and helping her clean up - despite her protests, she had it handled - we head up to the second floor to knock on Bellamy's door. When he doesn't answer, Juliet casts a spell which will tell us if anyone is currently in the room.

"I get nothing," she says, shaking her head.

"You gals have had a long day," Agnes tells us. "I think you'll find after a good night's sleep, the answers may come to you when you least expect it."

Considering Agnes has been right about everything else so far, and because I'm exhausted, I excuse myself to my room for some reading. With a mere two pages read, I'm fast asleep.

Chapter 11

"**P**sst! Psst! Wake up!"

"Huh? What?" I mumble through some wild dream that Wendy is trying to wake me up in the middle of the night while we're vacationing in Palisade.

"I found the enchanted orchard!" she hisses, her face way too close to mine for comfort. Never mind. It isn't a dream. Wendy really is waking me up in the middle of the night. Lucky for her, the moonlight streaming through the window illuminates her face, so I don't mistake her for a deranged killer.

"I thought I was dreaming?" I mumble. "How did you find the orchard?"

"Technically I didn't find it yet. But I have a map."

"There's a map?"

"It was in my room the entire time."

"I don't get it. Did you drink more peach wine than I realized?"

"No! Remember when we checked in? Agnes told us each room was special?"

"I think so. Can't this wait until morning?" I moan, placing the pillow over my head, and rolling away.

"No! Put some proper clothes on and I'll tell you on the way there."

"I'm sure I'll regret this, but wake up Juliet and I'll get dressed."

"I'm already here," Juliet whispers from the shadows.

Of course she is.

After changing into jeans and a t-shirt, still wondering if Wendy has finally lost it, we tiptoe downstairs, pausing at Harrison Bellamy's door, but it's dark. He must have come in after we went to bed. I make a note to myself to get up extra early to see if I can catch him in the morning.

Clara and Mystery are as surprised as I was to be awakened in the middle of the night. However, unlike me, they're thrilled we're going on an adventure.

"Where are we going?" Mystery asks, stretching long and hard in the way only a cat can.

"Wendy says she has a map to the enchanted orchard."

"Nice! Let's go."

"This is so exciting!" Clara squeals. "I love going on adventures with you girls."

I wish I was as excited as Mystery and Clara, but before I can protest further, we're following the map, with Wendy giving me step-by-step instructions.

When we reach the turnoff to enter the orchard, I start to regret this. Despite the balmy August night, I shiver while driving along the dark, twisting, turning road. Dense woods flank the sides of our path like silent sentinels guarding ancient secrets.

It reminds me too much of the time I was stranded on the side of Red Mountain, confident I was going to die at the hands of the bloody hook guy we told stories about at camp when we were teenagers.

The dim glow of the bus headlights cast eerie shadows on gnarled branches, stretching like skeletal fingers in our direction. Every bend leads us deeper into the heart of darkness.

"I swear, Wendy, if we get stranded out here and murdered by the bloody hook guy, I'll be so mad at you," I scold her.

"Are we there yet?" Mystery asks.

"Mystery is asking if we're there yet."

"Pretty soon," Wendy assures us.

"You still didn't tell me how you got the map."

"Remember how Agnes told us each room is special?"

"Yes, you already mentioned it."

"I think the room pointed out the map because it sensed I needed it."

"Go on," I tell her, still skeptical about how this map suddenly showed up.

"I left my window open when I went to bed because the faint breeze was so refreshing. I swear it smelled like peaches, too. But at some point, the breeze was strong enough to wake me up, and that's when I saw it."

"Don't tell me the map floated in your window."

"No, silly, now let me finish. The breeze was getting so strong it made this colorful tapestry hanging in my room, billow and sway. When I got up to close the window, light from the moon highlighted a hidden compartment behind the tapestry."

"No way."

"I'm serious. How else do you think I could find this?"

"Keep going," I sigh.

"I opened the compartment, assuming it would be empty, but lo and behold, there was a map."

"If you tell me the map had Enchanted Orchard written across the top, I'm turning the bus around."

"No, silly, but I know this is it. It's the enchanted orchard."

"So, we're driving along this dark scary road following what you *think* is a map to the enchanted orchard?"

"It's been right so far, hasn't it? I have a gut feeling this is it."

"We'll see about that."

"Okay, stop!" Wendy bellows.

"Where?"

"Here!"

"There's no here, here!"

"Whatever. Just stop. The map says stop," she insists.

"Now what?" I ask, after stopping the bus on the side of the road.

"We get out," Wendy says, but with far less confidence than she showed earlier.

"How will this help us find Evelyn's peach cobbler recipe?"

"I don't know!"

"I don't like this at all," Clara warns.

"We have flashlights, right? Let's explore for a bit, and if we don't see anything, we'll come right back. I promise," Wendy insists.

We pile out of the bus, a haunting silence filling the air, broken only by the distant hoot of an owl and leaves rustling under our feet. The wind whispers mournfully through the trees, carrying the faint scent of ripe peaches.

"Remember the scene in the Wizard of Oz when the trees talk and throw apples at Dorothy and her friends?" Juliet says.

She seriously had to bring that up now? It's one of the creepiest parts of the movie. "If these trees throw peaches at us, we're outta here, and we're leaving Wendy behind," I insist.

"Watch your step, ladies!" Clara calls from the bus. "It's dark out!"

"No kidding," I mutter, just as I slip on an overly ripe peach before plunging into a deep, dark hole. My screams of terror bring the others running. I'm not sure how far I fell. It felt like forever. I was prepared to break every bone in my body, but thankfully, something squishy broke my fall.

"Holly! Holly!" Juliet screams. "Are you there? Are you okay?"

"Holly!" Wendy also screams. "I'm so sorry! This is all my fault. Are you okay? Did you break anything?"

"I'm okay. I landed on something squishy," I call up. What seemed like a 10 foot hole as I was falling is probably more like half that. Hopefully I can get out on my own with a little help.

Unfortunately, I dropped my flashlight when I fell, and it's too dark to see where it landed. It's pitch black except for a sliver of moonlight shining on… "Dagnabit!" I swear.

"What is it?" Juliet calls down to me.

"It's a body!"

"A body! Are you sure?"

"Yes, the big chef's knife sticking out of his chest is a dead giveaway."

"Did you really just say dead?"

"I'm sitting on a body, and you're pointing out my pun?"

"Who is it?" Wendy asks.

"Hang on a second. I dropped my flashlight."

"Then how can you see a knife?"

"The moon, silly."

"Here it is!" I declare, the moment my hand grasps the cold steel of the flashlight, but when I switch it on, I kind of wish I hadn't.

"Who is it?" Wendy asks again.

"It's Harrison Bellamy!"

Chapter 12

"Can you help me out of here?" I beg. I've been closer to more dead bodies this year than I care to admit, and while they don't particularly freak me out - I talk to ghosts, after all - this is the first time I've fallen on one. I'm glad there was something to break my fall at least. But at the same time - ick! I just landed on a body.

Juliet and Wendy, their faces etched with concern, drop to their knees, peering into the dark hole as they strain to reach my outstretched hands. Clara calls out instructions from the bus, but of course, they can't hear her.

"Grab her hand and forearm if you can reach it," Juliet tells Wendy. "I have this side." After waiting for Wendy to secure her grip, she takes a deep breath. "On three," she says. "One, two, three," she exclaims while they desperately tug on me.

I brace my feet against the dirt walls, but it's slippery, and I falter, knocking against the side of the hole. A gust of air escapes my lips, creating a resonating whoosh that hangs in the air. The flimsy t-shirt I threw on offers little protection as my bare arms scrape painfully against the rough clay. I'm grateful I'm at least wearing jeans.

"One more time," Juliet says. "One, two, three," she grunts as they give it their all to pull me up.

My feet claw at the sides of the slippery hole, but when I discover a dense root, I leverage it to hoist myself out with a heave from my friends, breathing an enormous sigh of relief when my feet finally reach solid ground.

"Are you all right?" Juliet asks, checking me over.

The scraped skin on the back of my arms stings, and I'll feel the bruises tomorrow, but at least I'm in one piece. "Aside from a few scratches and bruises, I think I'm okay. Especially compared to the guy at the bottom of the hole. It would have been more exciting if you used witchcraft to pull me out, though," I lecture.

"Do you want us push you in and try again?" Wendy smirks.

"How about I just say thank you?" I tell them.

She smiles. "No problem, friend."

"All good, Clara!" I shout, raising my arms to show her I'm in one piece.

"Thank goodness!" she exclaims.

"I would have just jumped out," Mystery informs me.

"Does anybody have cell service out here?" I ask. Do enchanted orchards have cell towers?

"Actually, I do," Wendy says, peering at her phone.

"We have to call the police."

"I was afraid you'd say that," she says, dialing 911, giving them exact instructions on how to find us.

"You're sure it's Bellamy?" Juliet asks.

"I'm completely sure."

"You're sure he was stabbed?" she continues, her tone telling me she hopes I'm wrong.

I shine my flashlight into the hole, showing the stab wound and the knife. "Completely sure about that too."

With the police on their way, our silence hangs heavy in the air, each of us lost in our thoughts, the weight of everything we've experienced today pressing down on us. After what feels like an eternity, the tension breaks, and we all talk at once.

"Do you think Harold did this?"

"What about Evelyn?"

"Remember, Mystery and Clara saw him arguing with Marcus, too."

"What should we say when the cops get here?"

"What do you mean?"

"They'll ask how we know the victim."

"We only kind of do," I remind them.

"Now, what would Sheriff Mack say about that?" Wendy asks.

We experience a brief pause before our gazes lock; then we erupt with laughter, breaking the tension and releasing built-up strain. Wendy throws her arms across her chest, mimicking Sheriff Mack's favorite stance when he wants to intimidate us.

Juliet sighs loudly, pinching the bridge of her nose.

"Oh yeah, he does that one too!" we laugh.

"Why is it that whenever there's trouble, I can count on seeing you ladies?"

The laughter bubbles forth uncontrollably. In that moment, the weight of the situation lifts, allowing us some solace. It's a choice between laughing or crying, and for now, we choose laughter. I love these two women who have become friends - scratch that - they're the family I haven't had since I was a child. What would I do without them?

We're alerted to the approaching police cars by blue and red lights casting an ethereal glow on the surrounding trees, their shadows dancing and flickering with each pulsating flash. The alternating hues reflect off the gnarled branches and twisted foliage, painting the forest in an otherworldly palette in what has become an all too familiar scenario for us.

The laughing halts when the officer in the first car gets out to glare at us. "Is this a crime scene or a party?" he asks.

"We were just thinking of someone back home," Juliet says.

"So, you aren't from around here?" he asks.

"We're from Glenwood Springs. We're here for the festival."

"You're here for the festival, yet you're in the middle of nowhere at 2 AM with a body?" a serious-looking woman, who could be the female equivalent of Sheriff Mack, says while she approaches us. His tiny counterpart, anyway. I think she's five feet tall if she's lucky. However, from her expression alone, I doubt anyone challenges her. "I'm Gabriella Montgomery, Chief of Police. Have you folks been drinking?"

"No!" we exclaim at once.

She stares at us suspiciously, like she can't imagine what we'd be doing out here if we weren't partying. Or worse yet, killing someone.

"Which one of you discovered the body?"

"That would be me." I step forward while she regards my disheveled appearance with disdain.

"How did you discover him?"

"Uh, I landed on him."

"Landed on him?"

"I slipped and fell in the hole."

She glances at the hole. "How did you get out?"

"They helped me," I nod at Wendy and Juliet, grateful they didn't use witchcraft after all. We may make fun of Sheriff Mack and his uptight ways, but at least he knows us. Perhaps he knows us too well, but we don't have to worry about what he'll think of our paranormal gifts.

"Dispatch said you know the victim?" Chief Montgomery says.

"Not really."

"But you gave them his name."

"I mean, we don't know him, know him. He's staying at the Peach Blossom Inn & Retreat with us. I don't mean with *us*. I mean *with* us." I cringe as the nervous words tumble from my lips. There's nothing to be nervous about. We've done nothing wrong.

Chief Montgomery purses her lips. "Huge coincidence, don't you think?"

"I don't know?" I trail off. How am I supposed to answer something like that?

"You're staying in the same inn as this man, who you claim you don't know, and yet you find yourselves in the middle of the night, in the middle of nowhere, falling onto his lifeless body? It all seems rather convenient, wouldn't you agree? This raises some serious questions which demand serious answers."

Hold the phone. Is she accusing us of something? "Do you think we killed him?" I ask outright.

"Wouldn't you?" she snaps.

None of us breathes a word. Obviously, we didn't kill him, but Chief Montgomery doesn't see it that way.

"You'll have to come back to the station with us," she growls.

"Are we under arrest?" Juliet asks.

"I think we should continue this conversation back at the station so we can let the investigators and medical examiner do their jobs unobstructed. Why don't you leave your..." she glances about, flinching when she spots the pink bus, "uhhh bus here and I'll have an officer pick it up later."

"You can't leave us here!" Clara shouts.

"We should follow you to the station so you won't have to come back here. It makes it easier for you," I suggest, hoping she'll take note of how accommodating I'm being.

It doesn't work, though, because she only regards us more suspiciously than ever. "I swear we'll follow right behind you. Where will we go in a bright pink bus, anyway? It's not like it's easy to hide."

She ponders it for a moment. "Follow my officer to the police station. But no funny business!"

"Not even a small joke, I promise." When she glares at me, I wonder if a lack of humor is a prerequisite for law enforcement leadership. Although, with Sheriff Mack, it's fun to rile him up. This lady just scares me.

"Are you in trouble?" Clara asks when we pile into the bus. "It sounds like you're in trouble."

"I hope not," I mutter.

"Clara is worried we're in trouble," I tell the others.

"I think they just want us to go to the station to fill out a witness report," Juliet tells her.

"You should call Sheriff Mack," Clara says.

"Oh, he'd be thrilled to learn we're in trouble again," I groan. "The last thing we need is another of his *leave this to the police* lectures."

While following the officer back to the police station, Juliet asks, "What will we tell them?"

"I don't know." I shake my head.

"You should always tell the truth," Clara says.

"What if they ask us again about what we were doing in a peach orchard in the middle of the night? Considering they might think the truth is a little out there," Wendy says.

"Which part of the truth? The part where you were magically led to a map giving us directions to an enchanted orchard, or the part where our friend Evelyn was worried about her husband attacking Harrison Bellamy because he was blackmailing her?"

"We should totally run," Mystery says.

"For once, I'm almost inclined to agree with you," I tell her. "I don't see an easy way out of this. If we don't tell them everything we know, we look like suspects. But if we do tell them everything we know, Evelyn and Harold look like suspects."

"What if Harold really did kill Bellamy, though?" Wendy asks.

"I don't know," I unintentionally snap at her. "I just don't know." Did I make a mistake insisting Evelyn tell Harold what Harrison was doing to her? Is his blood on my hands?

"Well, we're about to find out," Wendy says as we follow the officer into the police station parking lot.

Great vacation so far.

Chapter 13

"Okay, girls, this is it. We have to stick together," I tell them as the officer we followed glares at us from the sidewalk, waiting for us to get out.

"It's not too late," Mystery begs. "Throw it in reverse and floor it!"

"Remind me to ask you some time what you did in your past life to make you so suspicious of authority figures," I tell her.

"Which one?" she laughs.

"Just tell the truth," Clara continues to urge me. "You can't go wrong with telling the truth."

I hop down from the driver's seat, taking in the Palisade Police Station. Like most small-town police stations, it sits in the middle of the community - a reminder of security and order.

The exterior is a traditional weathered brick facade, surrounded by a neatly manicured lawn and several strategically placed flower beds stuffed with colorful petunias, geraniums, and hydrangeas, albeit a bit wilted from the summer heat.

"This way, ladies," the officer says, gesturing along the walkway. He waits for us to go first, no doubt, in case we decide to run. Sturdy oak doors bearing large brass handles and the town emblem affixed to the center, secure the entrance. I swallow hard before grasping the thick handle and pulling.

I try not to think about how much trouble we're in. What if they don't believe us? What if we tell the truth and they laugh at us, or worse, lock us up and throw away the key? Sheriff Mack was skeptical when he first learned I talked to ghosts. I had to prove it to him. And if he realized how much we talked about him on this trip, he'd laugh himself silly. I admit, even he has become a friend to me since I moved to Glenwood Springs. But don't tell him I said that.

The lobby is surprisingly well lit for the middle of the night. Framed photographs of police officers, both historical and more recent, adorn the walls. Some contain awards, others feature pictures of the officers within the community. I detect the subtle scent of cleaning products enhanced by the hum of the night janitor polishing floors with a large buffer.

"Follow me, please," the officer says, leading us past the reception desk, down a long, lonely hallway. He unlocks the door to a room, which I can only assume is an interrogation room, before gesturing at us to go inside. If I weren't so nervous, I'd point out how it's exactly like I see on TV cop shows. There's a small, rectangular table surrounded by several chairs, recording equipment, and a one-way mirror. I stare at it, wondering if someone is behind it, staring back.

"Take a seat," he tells us, pointing to the chairs. When we each sit down without a peep, it hits me how uncharacteristically quiet it is for us. "Do you understand this conversation is being recorded?" he asks, switching on the camera.

"Yes," we tell him.

He takes out a pen and notepad before sitting across from us. "Start at the beginning. Why were you in the orchard at 2 AM?"

Wendy looks at me, and I nod. Clara is right. We're better off just telling the truth. If they judge us for being paranormal, then they just do.

"I found a map in my room at the Peach Blossom Inn," she starts, her voice shaking.

"A map to the orchard?"

"Yes."

"Do you always follow random maps you find in a bed-and-breakfast?"

"No, we were looking for an enchanted orchard," she says.

He pauses. "Come again?"

"We were told the enchanted orchard may hold clues," I interrupt.

"Clues to what?"

"To finding the..." I pause because I can't believe I'm about to say this out loud to a stranger.

"To finding the what?"

"To finding the Indigo Midnight Shifters and hopefully the Whitman's missing peach cobbler recipe."

"I'm aware of the missing recipe, because they filed a police report, but what else did you say you were looking for?"

"Indigo Midnight Shifters," I tell him.

He stares into my eyes unblinking, like he's trying to decide if I'm drunk or high or making it up on the spot. "What exactly is an Indigo Midnight Shifter?"

"I'm not entirely certain. I don't think I've ever met one."

"So, why were you looking for them?"

"Because Jasper McAlister told me they might lead to answers for the missing recipe."

"Who's Jasper McAlister?"

Oh, dear. "He's a ghost from the 1850s, I believe. Probably a gold miner who passed away here." I mumble as quickly as I can.

"Say what?"

I repeat what I just told him but with more conviction.

"Okayyy," he says, scribbling furiously on his notepad. When he catches me trying to read it, he moves the notepad closer, covering it with his arm like I'm trying to cheat on a grade school math test.

"Why were you hoping to locate the missing recipe in the first place?"

"The Whitmans hired us."

"Hired you?"

"Yes, sir." I nod.

"Why?"

"I'm a Paranormal Private Investigator."

When he sighs heavily while pinching the bridge of his nose, I bite my lip to keep from laughing. "I'm sure I'll regret this, but what does a Paranormal Private Investigator do?"

"A variety of things. But a lot of what I do involves talking to ghosts."

"Ghosts?"

"Yes, sir, I see dead people."

"Okay."

"And you two. You also see dead people?"

"No," Wendy shakes her head. "Spirit communicators are rare. I'm a potions witch."

"I see."

"And you?" he asks Juliet.

"I'm a sun witch."

"Wonderful. And you drive around in a bright pink VW bus solving mysteries?"

"Pretty much!" we all nod.

He sighs again, raking his hand through short, sandy blond hair. He and Sheriff Mack should have a drink together after this. "The medical examiner estimates the time of death around 11 PM. Also, when we dusted the knife for fingerprints, it appears to have been wiped clean. Can you tell me where you were around 11 PM?"

"I was asleep in the Peach Blossom Inn," I tell him.

"Me too!" Wendy nods while Juliet agrees with her.

"You said earlier, the victim, Harrison Bellamy, was also a guest at the inn."

"Yes." I nod.

"Did you speak to him at all?"

We shake our heads no.

"But you fell into the hole he was in, in this so-called enchanted orchard?"

"Yes."

"When was the first time you saw Harrison Bellamy?" he asks.

"At the inn when he was checking in," I tell him, but when Wendy gives a slight hiccup, I remember that the first time I actually saw him was when he was arguing with Evelyn. Rats. I forgot about that.

"What was that?" he points at Wendy. "You were about to disagree with her."

"I believe my friend Holly forgot that the first time we saw Harrison Bellamy..." she pauses, her brow wrinkling with worry.

"Go on."

"We saw him at Riverbend Park during the ice cream social."

"What was he doing?"

"He was arguing with Evelyn Whitman."

"What about?"

"We couldn't hear them. We were too far away."

She isn't lying, at least.

"Wait here," he says. "I'll be right back." When he pushes his chair back abruptly, I flinch at the unnaturally loud scraping noise.

Where is he going? Did I say something wrong? He's coming back with handcuffs and prison jumpsuits, isn't he? This can't be happening. I look awful in orange. Why didn't we run like Mystery suggested? My imagination blasts into overdrive, inventing numerous ways that he's going to torture the truth out of us, even though we've already told him the truth.

Given the expressions on Wendy and Juliet's faces, they must be thinking the same thing. None of us breathes a word because we're afraid they're watching and listening. After what seems like hours, but in reality is more like 20 minutes, the officer returns.

"You three are free to go."

When we gawk at him dumbfounded, he explains, "I called Agnes Plumfield. She confirms she saw each of you go to your rooms after dinner, and you were still there when she went to bed at 1 AM. She also confirmed your pink bus was parked in the same spot all night. She told me she saw Mr. Bellamy check-in, then go outside to get his luggage, but that was the last time she saw him."

Clara's news that they saw him arguing with Marcus Reynolds springs to mind, but I won't say anything just yet. What if Marcus stole the recipe? I need to make sure before I point fingers at anyone.

Just as we all begin to exit the door, the deputy grabs my arm. "I talked to Sheriff Mack at the Garfield County Sheriff's Department."

Juliet groans.

"He vouched for you. Said you're a pain in his rear and cause him more trouble than he's willing to admit, but that you're solid people who are incapable of murder. He added he wasn't the least bit surprised you fell in a hole."

When Wendy pauses to argue with the officer I pull her down the hallway. "Thank you," I tell him as we scurry back the way we came and out the door before he can change his mind.

It turns out we weren't in there all day like we thought. The sun is just now peeking over the horizon, its gentle rays spilling across the picturesque town, casting a warm glow onto vibrant streets. Palisade prepares for another day of the festival, unaware that one of their own may have committed murder overnight.

Meanwhile, I feel like Scrooge waking up on Christmas Day, realizing he still has a shot at redemption. Not that I need redeeming. Okay, maybe a little. Still. I want to dance a jig on the sidewalk, I'm so relieved. When Clara hangs out of the bus window cheering, I cheer back.

Wendy smirks in my direction. "Sooo, Sheriff Mack…"

"Don't even start!" I scold her.

Chapter 14

We pile out of the bus in front of the Peach Blossom Inn, breathing a collective sigh of relief. I've never been so happy to see a bed and breakfast in my life. As for what lies ahead, I prefer not to think about it for now. I'm starving and eager to see what Agnes has for breakfast. If it's anything like last night's meal, I'll have one of every-thing. Nope. Make that two.

"Welcome back!" Agnes cries. "How are you, my poor dears? I couldn't believe it when the police station called to tell me you found a body! And they were holding you for questioning! I told them under no circumstances did you have anything to do with a murder."

"Thank you for vouching for us," Wendy says, wrapping Agnes in a big hug. "It was a long night."

"They asked me when I last saw Harrison Bellamy?" Agnes says. "What's that about?"

"They didn't tell you?" How can she not know he's dead?

"They only said they questioned you about a murder. Oh no, oh, my goodness," she cries, placing her hand against her chest. "Don't tell me it was Harrison Bellamy!"

"I'm afraid it was."

"Oh, dear. I assume the police will be here shortly to search his room. I better warn the other guests. It won't do to have them frightened off by an unexpected visit from law enforcement."

"Is that breakfast I smell?" Wendy asks when we notice the aroma of sizzling bacon and eggs, cooked to perfection, wafting through the lobby.

"Yes, my dears, you must be famished. Head into the dining room and help yourselves."

I gasp in awe at the spread before us. Freshly squeezed juice and colorful fruit platters brimming with juicy peaches, cherries, and melons take up the center of the table. To the left of them, is an array of flaky peach danishes and buttery scones with a decorative jar of peach preserves nearby.

"Would you care for some peach pancakes?" the cook asks Wendy, who nods vigorously while he arranges a stack of fluffy pancakes topped with a dollop of whipped cream and a drizzle of maple syrup.

"What's that?" I point to an omelet pan.

"That is an avocado and goat cheese omelet, miss."

"What about this?" I point to something else. Everything looks so good. How will I ever decide?

"It's peach-infused French toast, caramelized to perfection, topped with a generous helping of fresh raspberries and a sprinkle of powdered sugar."

"Yes," I tell him.

"Yes, to..." he laughs.

"Yes, to everything!" I exclaim.

It isn't until after we've loaded our plates with all these delicious choices and plop down at the dining room table to dig in, I realize we haven't even changed our clothes. Oh well. I wouldn't pass up this breakfast for the world. A change of clothes can wait.

"So what's next?" Wendy asks with a mouthful of fruit. "Aside from finishing breakfast, of course."

"We haven't followed up on Marcus Reynolds' alibi, so that's our first stop," I explain.

"Do you really think Marcus could have killed Harrison Bellamy?" Juliet asks.

"We need to know why they were arguing," I remind them.

"What if he stole the recipe, and he and Bellamy fought over it, so he killed him?" Wendy gasps.

"I wouldn't be surprised." I shrug.

"Remember how nervous he was when we questioned him?" Juliet says. "What if he was already planning to kill Bellamy, then?"

"I guess we'll find out soon," I tell her, right before shoveling a forkful of omelet in my mouth.

After breakfast, we retreat to our rooms to shower and change. When I agreed to look for the stolen recipe, I certainly didn't realize it would turn into a murder investigation on top of it.

"Phew! I feel so much better!" Wendy exclaims when we meet downstairs. "Prison changes a person, you know."

"You were a visitor at the police station for about five minutes," Juliet reminds her.

"In prison time, it's equal to like five years," Wendy sighs.

"All right, my fellow inmates, first stop. Freshest Harvest Express!" I exclaim, firing up the bus.

"What's happening now?" Clara asks.

"We're following up on Marcus Reynolds' alibi."

"That dude looked super shifty," Mystery says.

"Yes, Juliet reminded us of how nervous he was when we questioned him."

"Don't forget, we saw him arguing with the man who was killed," Clara says.

"Are you sure you didn't hear anything?" I ask.

"Not a word."

"Did it get physical in any way?"

"You mean, did they scratch each other's eyes out?" Mystery says while swiping her paw through the air, making exaggerated meowing noises.

"Kind of?"

"Nope. None of that," she tells me. "Just in each other's faces and arguing."

Freshest Harvest Express is a sprawling industrial complex on the town's edge. It has an earthy scent of ripe fruits and crisp vegetables. Trucks and vans adorned with vivid logos and painted images of vibrant produce come and go while forklift operators deftly navigate the area, loading and unloading produce pallets.

"Looks like we're supposed to check in there," Wendy says, pointing to a sign leading us to the front office.

"Good morning! Welcome to Freshest Harvest Express! How may I help you?" a bubbly young receptionist dressed in the company uniform greets us. Neatly styled blonde hair frames her face, while a name badge pinned to her lapel identifies her as Emma.

"Hi Emma, we're here to see Frank," I tell her, holding up the business card Marcus gave us.

"Certainly, right away."

As we wait for Frank, Wendy pokes me repeatedly. "What is it?" I finally ask in frustration.

She points to a large window where several people are chopping produce into smaller sections using large chef's knives.

"We may not know about Marcus' motive," I whisper. "But there's our means."

"Hi there, how can I help you?" a tall, well-built man who carries himself with an air of confidence, and who I assume is Frank, approaches us. His tailor-fitted suit, neatly trimmed dark beard, and piercing gaze give him a distinguished appearance. Yet his warm smile makes him seem personable and approachable.

"Yes, I have a question about something that happened yesterday morning, which delayed your delivery drivers."

"I apologize for the most unfortunate incident. It was completely unexpected. Did you folks have trouble with an order?"

"No, it's not that at all. I'm a Paranormal Private Investigator working on behalf of Evelyn Whitman. Marcus Reynolds told us he was late for his delivery at the Dough & Tell yesterday and he gave us your name to confirm his story."

"Marcus is one of my best employees, and I promise you, the only reason he was late was due to the accident at the docking station.

"So you can confirm he was here most of the morning?"

"I can. He's not in trouble, is he? I'd really hate to lose him."

"No, not at all." Unless he murdered Harrison Bellamy, of course. "We were just following up on our investigation. We appreciate your time. Is Marcus around by chance?"

"He should be returning from his morning run at any moment. You're welcome to stay if you'd like."

"Thank you so much! I think we will."

"So that rules him out as the one who stole the recipe, at least," Juliet points out.

"But not the murderer," Wendy says. "Did you see how big those knives were?"

"I wish I paid more attention to what the knife looked like. Although with it buried in Harrison's chest, I didn't really have the chance. But it was definitely a big knife. It looks like he just pulled up."

"Hey, Marcus!" I wave at him as we approach his truck.

"Uhhh, hello?" he half-heartedly waves back.

"We met yesterday. We asked you about the Whitmans and their peach cobbler recipe."

"Yeah, sure. You went and had a chat wit my boss, huh?"

"We did. He confirmed you were here helping clean up from the accident at the docking station."

"You need anyting else?"

"We saw you arguing with Harrison Bellamy outside the Peach Blossom Inn right before yesterday's rainstorm. Can you tell us what you were fighting about?"

"Not sure dat's any of your business. Why don't you ask him?"

"We can't. He's dead."

Unmistakable relief flashes across his face. "Dat Bellamy guy is dead? Well, I'll be a grasshopper's cousin. Wait a second; you tink I did it?"

"We'd just like to know why you were arguing."

"I don't see how dat's important."

"It's important because the police are investigating this as well, and you can either answer our questions or you can answer theirs. Who would you rather have here, us or the police?"

Yes, I feel a little bit guilty we're manipulating him into fessing up. I doubt the police even know about Marcus and Harrison. Clara and Mystery may have been the only ones who saw them argue, given that everyone else was desperate to get out of the impending storm.

"I'll tell you what you need tah know cuz I don't need no cops around here got it?" he says while we nod enthusiastically.

"Harrison Bellamy wanted tah pay me tah steal the recipe. I told him nuttin doin. I don't need dat kinda trouble. When I refused his money, he blackmailed me."

"How did he blackmail you?"

He sighs heavily, looking this way and that to ensure no one overhears him.

"At 18, I was nuttin but trouble. High school dropout, my old man was a drunk, my mom took off years before. I worked some odd jobs here and dere, picking up trash, hauling junk, dat sort of thing. Most days, though, I did nuttin but sit around, get high, and watch TV.

One night I got into a bar fight. It was stupid, really. Some jerk was messing wit dese ladies at the bar, and like an idiot, I told him tah knock it off. So what does he do? He breaks dis beer bottle on dah bar and cut me with it." He pauses, pointing to a long, jagged scar on his chin. "He said he was gonna slit my throat. So I punched him. But den he fell backward and hit his head causin brain damage! I got sent away for five years for assault. The weirdest thing is, prison was dah best ting to ever happen."

When I notice Wendy nodding at him like she completely gets it, I swat at her arm. You just wait. The story of our brief time in the police station will only get bigger and more exaggerated over time.

"It's where I learned tah read and got my GED. I was all set to walk the straight and narrow. Get a good job and all dat, you know. But when I go to apply for jobs, I gotta tell em I'm a felon. Guess where dat got me? No where!" he exclaims. "I finally paid a guy $300 for a social security number, changed my name, and I been Marcus Reynolds ever since. Not a single bit of trouble since den. Never even called in sick to work."

"But Harrison Bellamy knew about your past."

"He sure did. I told him Evelyn Whitman is a nice lady and I ain't stealin no recipe. Besides, she keeps it in a safe and I couldna get to it even if I wanted to."

"Hold up. She told us she and Harold were the only ones who knew it was in the safe."

Marcus laughs. "Anybody who visited dat back room on dah regular like I did knew dah recipe was in dah safe. They ain't exactly quiet about it."

"Did anyone other than the Whitmans know the combination?"

"Beats me! Bellamy told me if I didn't figure out how to steal the recipe, he'd snitch to my boss about my fake paperwork. Sure, I hated the guy, but if I wouldn't even steal a recipe, why would I kill someone?"

"Just one more question. Where were you at 11 PM last night?"

"I was helping clean out Riverbend Park after dah storm. Sometimes I pick up work for the city for a little extra dough. I shovel snow, mow lawns, or like yesterday, clean up tree branches. You're not gonna tell my boss, are ya? I can't afford to lose my job. I don't wanta go back to jail neither."

"Nah. Our main concern is finding the recipe. But if you hear anything more about it, can you get in touch? We're staying at the Peach Blossom Inn & Retreat," I tell him.

"Sure ting, lady! Thanks for not rattin' me out."

Chapter 15

"Where to next, boss?" Wendy asks.

"It's time we talk to Evelyn and Harold again."

"But what if Harold killed Harrison?" Juliet points out in her usual worried tone.

"Then we urge him to confess to the police."

"What if he's dangerous?" she presses.

"I don't think he's dangerous. Not to us anyway. I still partly blame myself if he did kill Harrison. Considering I'm the one who insisted Evelyn tell him about Bellamy. Even if he killed Harrison, maybe it was an accident, or a crime of passion. He has no reason to kill us."

"Uh oh, check it out!" Mystery says as we approach the Dough & Tell Bakery.

I slow to a crawl, driving past the bakery, staring at the three cop cars parked haphazardly in front, their lights still flashing, and doors open. They definitely aren't here for pastries. This is so bad. My heart pounds in my chest and a knot of anxiety gathers in my stomach while I desperately search for a parking spot. My chest tightens while my mind races with worry and uncertainty. There could be 100 reasons the cops are at the Dough & Tell, but none good.

Eventually, I find a parking spot down the street. Wendy and Juliet practically jump out of the VW before I can bring it to a complete stop. I sprint after them, berating myself for insisting Evelyn tell Harold about Harrison. What if Harold killed him, and the police figured it out already? I told them I saw Evelyn arguing with Harrison. They could have put the pieces together to figure out what he did. Or maybe he confessed!

Or what if Harold killed Evelyn after she told him what had happened? He wouldn't do something like that, would he? I can barely stand to think about it.

We cluster with the other looky loos around the yellow crime scene tape while I press against it hoping to get a better view.

"Step back, please ma'am," a police officer tells me.

"What's going on? I'm a friend of the family. I need to know what's happening."

"Official police business, ma'am."

"Harold!" I cry out when he appears at the door in handcuffs. "Harold! Where's Evelyn?"

Please, please, please tell me he didn't do anything to Evelyn.

"Holly!" Harold shouts as he struggles to make his way over to us, but the police officer holds him back. "C'mon guys, just let me talk to her. You've known me forever. Joey, we went to high school together. Cut me some slack."

When Joey reluctantly agrees, Harold runs over to us. "You have to go to the festival. Evelyn is holding a press conference. You have to stop her!"

"But why are they arresting you?"

"Just promise me you'll go to the park to stop Evelyn!"

"Harold! Why are they arresting you?" I repeat.

"They say I killed Harrison Bellamy!"

"You didn't?"

"Of course not! I didn't even know he was dead," he insists. "But they found a knife that doesn't even belong to me in the kitchen and a spot of Harrison's blood on my apron."

When I stare back at him skeptically, he pleads. "I swear, Holly. I didn't do it, but that's not important right now. You have to stop, Evelyn. She'll ruin her life."

Wait, did Evelyn kill Harrison? Is that what she's planning to say at the press conference? I wouldn't have predicted that.

"Holly, come here," he says, so I lean forward, eager to learn what he has to say.

"I stole the recipe," he whispers in my ear.

"Come again?"

"I stole the recipe," he says a little louder.

"You stole your own recipe?" I hiss back.

"I already knew what Bellamy was doing. I decided the safest option was for the recipe to go missing. But on purpose, of course."

"But it's a crime to make a false report," I point out.

"I never intended to report it."

"But you were willing to let Evelyn think the recipe was really stolen?" That's harsh.

"No! Of course not! But I didn't realize that Evelyn had skipped the bank the day before. I had every intention of telling her before she noticed it was gone."

"Let me get this straight. You knew Bellamy was black-mailing Evelyn?"

"Yes! I worried we'd never get rid of him, so I came up with a plan to pretend the recipe was stolen. I was sure once he realized the recipe was gone, he'd give up and leave. But then Evelyn noticed the recipe was gone before I could tell her. Then you ladies showed up, and next thing I know, we're reporting the theft. I was in way over my head. When Evelyn told me about Bellamy yesterday, I told her about the recipe. You have to believe me. I never meant for this to get so out of control. Now Evelyn is at the festival holding a press conference."

"About what?"

"I don't know. She just left a note for me saying she was confessing everything at the festival at noon."

"We have to get to the park. Now!" I tell Wendy and Juliet.

"Where are you going?" Clara cries as we sprint down the street. It's faster to run there on foot than it will be to drive the VW and try to find parking again.

"I'll tell you everything later! Don't go anywhere!" Why did I just say that? Of course they aren't going anywhere. Although they'd steal the bus in a heartbeat if they could.

My mind races as we sprint to the park to keep Evelyn from confessing, even though I don't know what she's confessing to in the first place. She must have killed Harrison. Where else would the knife and blood come from?

Evelyn is confessing while Harold is being arrested, and the recipe was never actually stolen in the first place. What a mess. It's my fault for getting involved with this. If only I'd turned her down to begin with, Harold could have told her what really happened, Harrison would have left town, and none of this would be happening right now.

Our footsteps echo with desperation as we run all out to get to the park on time. Eventually, the park comes into view, along with a crowd gathered around the main stage, where Evelyn is preparing to talk. But where are the police? Maybe they don't know what Evelyn is confessing to either.

When we push through the crowd, Wendy cries out, "Evelyn! Evelyn!" her voice carrying above the crowd's murmurs. "Wait!"

Evelyn turns, her eyes widening in surprise when she sees us maneuvering through the sea of people to reach her. Her expression is a mix of confusion and concern, but she makes no move to leave the stage.

"We need to talk to you!" I plead, my voice cracking with emotion. "Please, just give us a moment."

I see Lillian nearby, looking ultra-smug. *She* obviously knows what Evelyn is about to confess. Even though we've only been in Palisade a short time, it's painfully clear the rivalry between Evelyn and Lillian is fierce. I can't help but feel a surge of anger toward her. She's the most disagreeable person.

When our eyes lock briefly, I sense the animosity emanating from her. She clearly takes delight in Evelyn's vulnerability, relishing the opportunity to see her competitor's downfall.

"What's she doing here looking all smug?" Wendy hisses at me.

"That's exactly what she's doing here. Gloating."

"She knows what Evelyn's about to confess to," Juliet says. "Doesn't she?"

"I was thinking the same thing." I nod.

But just as I approach Lillian to give her a piece of my mind, Evelyn clears her throat near the microphone.

No! Someone stop her!

"Thank you all for being here today. I have called this press conference to address a matter of utmost importance, one that weighs heavily on my heart. It is with a mixture of humility and regret that I must reveal a truth that has been hidden for far too long."

I glare at Lilian who continues to look self-righteous while the rest of the crowd appears confused.

"As many of you are aware, my family has been known for our award-winning peach cobbler recipe for generations. We have always taken great pride in this cherished family tradition, passing down the recipe from one generation to the next. However, it is with a heavy heart that I must confess, thanks to some unexpected discoveries, I now realize my ancestors stole the peach cobbler recipe over 150 years ago--"

"What?" Lillian shrieks. "You've got to be kidding me!"

"You guys, Lillian is genuinely shocked. She didn't expect her to say that."

"She thought she was confessing to murdering Harrison," Juliet says.

Evelyn continues. "I stand before you today, not to justify or defend these actions, but to take responsibility for the truth and to honor the legacy of those who truly deserve recognition. It is my sincere hope that by coming forward with this confession, we can begin the process of making amends and acknowledging the rightful origins of this beloved recipe.

I humbly ask for your understanding and support during this time of reflection and growth. I'm happy to answer any questions you might have."

Uh. Oh. She shouldn't have said that.

"Evelyn! Evelyn! Do you know who stole the recipe yesterday?" a reporter shouts.

"Uhhh..." Evelyn stammers. Now that she knows the truth, what can she say?

"Don't you think it's ironic that your ancestors stole the recipe and now someone has stolen it from you?"

"Uhhh, well..."

This is not going well.

"Hey, where's Lillian?" I whisper.

"I don't know. She was here a second ago," Wendy says.

"Evelyn, what do you think of your husband murdering Harrison Bellamy?"

"Excuse me?" Evelyn laughs nervously. "Is that your idea of a joke?"

"No, ma'am. The police just arrested him."

Chapter 16

The crowd gasps, their faces contorting with disbelief and surprise. Murmurs and whispers ripple throughout while they exchange glances, trying to process the unexpected revelations. Evelyn stands frozen, her eyes wide with astonishment. She stutters to find the words to respond.

Some begin to mutter their doubts, refusing to believe the accusation of murder, but wondering if the story about the recipe is accurate. Others exchange worried looks, unsure how to react to such grave news. Harold and Evelyn are well known throughout this town; how could Evelyn lie about the recipe, and Harold murder someone?

The festival's atmosphere quickly shifts from excitement to somber and tense. Reporters and bystanders alike bombard Evelyn with questions. Still, others back away in disbelief, as if removing themselves from the situation will make everything okay again.

Juliet runs onto the stage to console Evelyn, followed by Wendy and me. Eventually, we steer her away from the crowd, where we find a hiding spot behind a festival booth to regroup. The sudden turn of events leave Evelyn visibly shaken. Her hands tremble while clutching Juliet's arm for support.

"I can't believe this is happening," she sobs, her voice laden with shock and distress. "Harold... arrested for murder? It's impossible. There must be some mistake. And Harrison Bellamy is dead? I don't understand any of this."

So much for my theory that Evelyn killed Harrison. Either that, or she's one heck of an actress. Her shock certainly appears genuine.

"Where is Harold right now? I have to see him. Take me to him," she begs.

"We saw him right before we got to the park. The police were taking him into custody," Juliet explains.

"This can't be happening. Harrison Bellamy is dead? Where? How?"

"The medical examiner said he was killed at 11 PM last night. I realize this will sound indelicate, but where were you and Harold at 11:00?"

"We were in the bakery talking. After you left, we told each other everything. Harold took the recipe to keep it safe because he knew Bellamy was blackmailing me."

"Yes, he told us that part. Did anyone see you in the bakery at 11:00? Can anyone vouch for you?" I press.

"I don't think so. Can you take me to the police station? I have to see Harold."

"Yes, of course. I'm not sure if they'll let us see him though…. but we can certainly try," I add when she appears ready to launch into a fresh round of tears.

The festival continues buzzing about the drama everyone just witnessed, giving us a chance to sneak Evelyn down a back alleyway undetected, where we return to the bus. It's only a few blocks to the police station, but easier to hide Evelyn from the media if we drive.

"Here we are," I tell her, opening the passenger side door while she continues clinging to Juliet like she's a liferaft amid a turbulent storm at sea.

"Who is this?" Mystery asks after we help Evelyn into the bus.

"This is Evelyn Whitman," I tell her before turning to Evelyn. "You'll find this hard to believe, but my spirit roommates are in the bus with us," I explain when she stares at me in confusion.

"Oh, that's nice," she murmurs. She's so distracted she doesn't even care.

"Where are we going?" Clara asks.

"We're taking Evelyn to the police station."

"Oh, to see her husband. By the way, the woman you met at the park, the one who you said could be a suspect in the recipe theft…"

"Yes! Did you see her?"

"She was hiding in the crowd while you were at the park."

"The crowd?"

"Yes, the crowd watching the police at the Dough & Tell."

"What was she doing?"

"I told you she was hiding," Clara says like it's the most obvious thing in the world.

"That's it?"

"Yes, she mostly kept to the back of the crowd and watched. But after a while, she ran up the street and disappeared."

I won't repeat Clara's words to Evelyn. I don't know what this means and don't want to worry her further. She has enough on her plate as it is.

When I slide into the parking spot in front of the police station, Wendy sighs. "Sooo we meet again, eh slammer."

"This is hardly the slammer!" I grit my teeth.

"It's like a full circle moment for me, you know?"

"Dramatic much?" Juliet sighs.

"Do you think they'll let me see him?" Evelyn asks.

"Hard to say. Hopefully, if we ask nicely, they will."

As luck would have it, we didn't even have to ask. Once inside, we see Harold sitting in a chair just behind the counter.

"Harold!" Evelyn cries. "Are you all right?"

"Sweetheart! I'm okay. I'm waiting for them to process me. What happened at the park? What did you say?"

"Why did they arrest you?" she exclaims, ignoring his question.

He shrugs. "I was minding my own business when the police burst through the front door shouting at me to back away from the pie crust I was rolling. I was so scared I thought I'd have a heart attack. They said they had a search warrant based on an anonymous tip. They went directly to the shelf where we keep the extra cutting boards and pulled out a knife that isn't even mine. It's like they knew right where to go, even though I don't keep knives there to begin with. I've never even seen that knife and I have no idea how it got there. But they said it was the same kind of knife that was used to stab Bellamy with."

"You're sure it isn't yours?" I ask.

"Of course, I'm sure. I don't use that brand of knives."

"What kind of knife did the police find?"

"A CulinaryEdge 3000."

"What's the difference?" Wendy asks while Evelyn, Harold, and Juliet look aghast.

"I prefer German steel for my knives," Harold says while Juliet nods enthusiastically.

"Knives are personal to a chef," she insists.

"And the CulinaryEdge 3000?" I ask, still not understanding the difference.

"It's made with Japanese steel," Harold explains.

"Okay?" Wendy says, still obviously confused over the fuss.

"German steel lasts longer. Better balanced," Juliet explains while mimicking a chopping motion.

"But what about the blood?" I ask.

"I can't explain it. I don't know how his blood got on the apron."

"Did you see blood when you put it on?"

"I wasn't wearing it. It was hanging on a hook on the door."

"You're being framed!" Evelyn insists.

"I agree." I nod. "Especially when it comes to this so called anonymous tip. You're sure that's what they said?"

"Yes," Harold insists. "It stood out as strange to me. But when I asked them where they got the tip, they ignored me."

When an officer finally comes to take Harold away for processing, Evelyn insists on staying even though we offer to take her home. "You can track down who did this to my Harold, can't you?" she begs.

"We'll certainly try," I tell her with more confidence than I feel.

I wait until we get outside to talk. "I didn't want to say anything in front of the Whitmans but after Harold mentioned the CulinaryEdge 3000 I remembered when Lillian gave us the peach cobbler, the pie server she used had the letters CE on the handle. It can't be a coincidence, right?"

"You think Lillian murdered Bellamy and framed Harold?" Juliet asks.

"Don't you?"

"But why would she kill Bellamy?"

"That's what we need to find out."

"Why do you think Lillian took off right after Evelyn said her family stole the recipe?" Wendy asks.

"I'm not sure," I respond, my brow furrowed. "It was clear Evelyn's confession caught Lillian off guard. It's like she expected her to confess to something entirely different. Evelyn and Harold and, of course, Harrison knew Evelyn's ancestors stole the recipe, but Lillian didn't."

"So, what kind of confession was she expecting?"

"That either Evelyn or Harold were accused of murder, is my guess," I tell them.

"Lillian was the only one, aside from us, who knew Harrison Bellamy was dead!" Juliet exclaims excitedly.

"We have to find her. If she killed Harrison and then framed the Whitmans for it, there's no telling what she could do next," I warn.

"She probably took off. She could be halfway through Utah by now," Wendy insists.

"No, I don't think she is. Getting away with murder isn't enough. Especially if the investigation reveals the Whitmans didn't murder Bellamy. Lillian wants revenge and given what she told me at the ice cream social I think she plans to sabotage the peach supply. That would be the ultimate revenge for a town that consistently ranked her second to Evelyn."

"Wait, what did she say at the ice cream social?"

"At the time I took it as an offhand comment. I just chalked it up to blowing off steam but now I'm worried she'll carry through with her threat. At this point she has nothing to lose."

"What did she say?" Wendy asks, bouncing up and down with nervous energy.

"Something like, if the town's peaches ceased to exist, so would the town."

Chapter 17

"How can we find Lillian?" Wendy asks, still a ball of nervous energy.

"Genevieve," I say, simply, although I'm surprised her name popped into my head.

"Genevieve? What does she have to do with this?" Juliet asks.

"Remember how she told us the enchanted peach blossom would guide us when we least expect it?"

"Of course. But how does that lead us to Lillian?"

"I can't explain it, but I think Genevieve is somehow more connected to all of this than we first thought."

"Connected as in guilty? Do you think she and Lillian are in on this together?" Wendy asks in shock.

"No, of course not. But like Agnes, she *knows* things."

"Do you think she's still at the festival?" Juliet asks.

"We're running out of time. We have to do something," Wendy urges.

"Let's go!" I exclaim.

As we approach her booth, Genevieve turns to us, a knowing smile gracing her lips. "Welcome, dear friends. I sensed you were coming. You wish to find Lillian, yes?"

Ha! I was right. She has answers. And just this once I let myself believe they'll be easy answers. Yes, I'm probably wrong, but I'll cling to my delusions as long as I can; thank you very much. "The town's peach supply is at stake," I tell her, hoping she won't think I'm completely off my rocker.

"I understand," she replies, her eyes flickering with concern. "As I told you last time, my dear, the enchanted peach blossom will guide you. You must trust its magic."

"But how does it work?" I ask, my impatience showing. Would it be rude to ask for an instruction manual? This would be so much easier if she'd give us step-by-step instructions.

"Your blossom holds the wisdom of the orchard and maintains a unique connection to those seeking truth and justice. That's how it found its way to you in the first place. With uncertainty clouding your minds and your dire need for answers, if you let it, you will feel its presence resonate within you, urging you toward truth."

"But what if we can't decipher its message?" I ask, looking to Juliet and Wendy for help. Why aren't they as frustrated as I am?

"Trust in the bond between the three of you," Genevieve urges. "Your friendship is a powerful force. Believe in it and you'll uncover the answers you seek. Use the enchanted peach blossom as a guide, a symbol of hope and unity. Embrace its light and let it lead you on your journey."

Genevieve sighs when I stare back at her blankly. As witches, Juliet and Wendy are much better at this than I am. I prefer concrete answers.

"I suspect the two of you already have a sense of how this must work," she says softly, nodding at Juliet and Wendy, "when the time comes, simply close your eyes and hold the blossom in your hand," she instructs. "Let your intentions be known, and it will reveal the path you must follow. Now, if you'll excuse me, I have some other customers who need my help."

"But!" I call out – it's too late. She's off talking to someone else. Couldn't she at least give us an address?

"You're the witches here. What do we do now?" I ask my friends.

"We have to return to the enchanted orchard," Juliet insists.

"I was afraid you would say that," I sigh.

"Why?"

"Because one of us fell on a dead body last time we were there," I remind them.

"So, watch where you're going this time," Wendy says.

"I'll have you know I slipped. And it was dark! Are you sure we have to do this again?" I ask. But when they stare at me, full of resolve, I realize I'm fighting a losing battle here. "Please tell me you still have the map."

"Sure do." Wendy waves it about.

"And the peach blossom?"

"In my pocket."

"Then back to the orchard it is."

Thankfully, in the daylight, the enchanted orchard is vastly different from last night. The dancing, eerie shadows give way to vibrant colors. The ancient trees and their branches, heavy with peaches, sway gently in the soft breeze.

Birds sing joyfully from their perches, transforming the mysterious and haunting atmosphere into an almost secret sanctuary where nature and magic converge. This hardly seems like a place for a murderer to hide out, plotting the town's demise.

What if the blossom and the map are wrong? And what about Genevieve? What if this is all a hoax? What if Genevieve and Lillian are in this together? As usual, I start to doubt myself, letting my imagination run straight to the dark places.

"I don't think any of this is working," I tell them. "Don't get me wrong. I like that it's not nearly as scary as last night, but what are we doing here? Is the magic peach blossom saying anything?"

I'm beginning to think of it like a magic 8-Ball. Ask it a question, shake it, then see what pops up. Not exactly a harbinger of truth. But when Wendy pulls the blossom from her pocket, delicately unwrapping it from the handkerchief, I'm shocked to see it's glowing. When did that happen?

"I think we're headed in the right direction," Wendy whispers.

"Ask it which way we should go first," I whisper back while Wendy and Juliet glare at me.

"Okay, okay, sorry. I don't always understand how magic works," I remind them. Ghosts, yes. Magic, no. But then it hits me. This is what Genevieve meant when she said our friendship was unique. Between my ability to communicate with spirits, and my friends' ability to harness magic, we make a powerful team.

"This way," Wendy whispers.

The journey into the enchanted orchard takes an unexpected turn as the foliage grows denser, and the once-filtered sunlight dims to a mere glimmer. There's a subtle shift in the atmosphere, as if the essence of the orchard is closing in around us. Each step we take plunges us deeper into its mysterious heart, and I'm worried we've strayed too far from the beaten path. I cling to Juliet and Wendy, hoping if we run into trouble, they'll know what to do.

A moment later, Juliet raises her fist, signaling us to stop. Only yards away, Lillian stands amidst a row of trees, her eyes intense and focused as she softly chants an incantation I can't understand.

"She's surrounded by the darkest aura I've ever seen," Juliet whispers as the ground trembles beneath our feet.

I shiver. Partly from the chill of the dark forest and partly from fear. It's one thing for us to chase down and tackle a bad guy with a fire extinguisher, like we did recently, but this is different. This is magic. Dark magic. And I don't know what to do.

"What is she saying?" I ask.

"She's cursing the orchard," Wendy says. "She's ensuring no peaches ever grow in this town again."

"Do something!" I hiss at them, thinking about trying to tackle her anyway, when Wendy and Juliet, anticipating my next move, hold me back.

"Don't! You can't stop it like that. You'd have to use a counterspell," Wendy says.

"Well, what's the counterspell?"

"I don't know!" Wendy exclaims.

"What do you mean you don't know? You're a witch. You're both witches!" I insist, my voice rising to near shriek level. Don't they memorize these things?

As Lillian's spell energy builds, the ground beneath us shakes, the livelihood of the enchanted orchard wavers in the balance. The atmosphere is heavy, almost angry. An eerie mist rises from the ground, enveloping the once vibrant trees.

If Wendy and Juliet think I'm going to sit here while Lillian destroys a town, they're out of their minds. But when I attempt to shake off their grip, they hold me tighter.

"Look!" Juliet points to a swirling turquoise-colored mist in the distance.

I've seen plenty of ghosts in my time. Some gruesome looking ones, like the one with the ax in his head or the one who was eaten by a shark - bleah, let's not even go there - but these beings are entirely different.

They stand tall and graceful, plus Juliet and Wendy can see them so they aren't ghosts. Their skin glows with a subtle luminescence, giving off an iridescent shimmer changing from deep indigo to midnight blue. Their eyes are large and captivating, with shades of silver, sapphire, and amethyst.

"Indigo Midnight Shifters!" I whisper in awe.

Chapter 18

T hey silently close in from all directions, their eyes glowing with primal intensity. One of them, who appears to be the leader, advances, her eyes never wavering from Lillian. Her long, silver hair shimmers in the faint light. When she raises her hands, a soft glow flows from her fingertips, forming a protective barrier throughout the orchard.

She then calls upon the spirits of the orchard (at least, that's what I hope she's doing) to rise against Lillian's dark magic. The earth beneath us rumbles in response, while the trees almost lean in like they're lending strength to the shifters.

Lillian's eyes widen in surprise and frustration as her spell meets resistance. She chants louder; her voice heavy with desperation and fear. Shadows flicker and dance around her, but the Indigo Midnight Shifters stand firm, their collective power growing with every passing moment.

While the magic unfolds in front of us, my heart races, the air is chill, and the hair on the back of my neck stands like never before. Just like Jasper said it would. I can scarcely believe my own eyes. There's a fusion of darkness and light, power and vulnerability, excitement and fright, all bound together in an intricate dance of magic. Clara will be so mad she missed this.

With a force of brilliance, the shifters counter Lillian's dark spell, creating a blinding display of light and color, pushing back the malevolent mist and dark energy. The enchanted orchard seems to come alive as if rejoicing in the impending victory.

In a final act of defiance, Lillian attempts to unleash one last surge of power, but the combined efforts of the shifters prove too much for her. With a flagging burst of energy, her spell falters, dissolving into the air, the orchard ultimately untouched by her evil.

"Noooooo!" she screams as the spell collapses and her black aura dissipates, leaving her with nothing but anger and defeat. She flails about desperate to retrieve her spell energy, but it's useless. The Indigo Midnight Shifters destroyed her plans.

"It's over! It's all over!" she cries out, her voice drenched with defeat and frustration as she pounds on the ground. Her screams echo throughout the orchard, their weight heavy with the failure of her malicious ambitions. Her dreams of sabotaging the town's peach supply and achieving a twisted victory lay crumbled at her feet. What a stark contrast to the smirking, cunning woman I saw at the park such a short time ago.

When she finally sees us gawking at her, she tries to run away, but the spell has left her exhausted, her movements feeble and unsteady, where she ultimately collapses into a heap on the ground. Her limbs sprawl across the orchard floor while she gasps for breath. Her resolve, which appeared unyielding only moments ago, is gone.

"I hope you're happy now!" she snarls. "You've ruined everything. All my dreams shattered because of your meddling."

I realize this is hardly the moment for laughter, but I want to so badly. If only she'd said, I'd have gotten away with it if it hadn't been for you kids... it would have been even more perfect.

"The police are on their way, Lillian. Why don't you tell us what happened?" Wendy says.

"Why should I tell you?"

"Because it's over. We know you didn't steal the peach cobbler recipe, but you did kill Harrison Bellamy and try to frame the Whitmans for it. It's just a matter of time before the truth comes out, anyway."

"You're right," she says, throwing her hands up, her dirt and tear-streaked face glowering at us with disdain. "I killed him! I killed Harrison Bellamy. He's been sniffing around here for years, trying to get the Whitmans," she snorts derisively, "or whoever the recipe actually belongs to, to sell to him. One day I thought, hey, he should buy *my* recipe! You've tasted it; you said it was delicious, right?" Lillian points at Wendy, who's nodding vigorously.

Yes, her peach cobbler was fabulous, but let's not encourage her. Her experience with the shifters has left her quite unhinged.

"I take second place to Evelyn every single year," she pounds on the dirt for emphasis, "even though mine is clearly better, so he should buy my recipe, right? But do you know what he said to me? Huh? Do you?" she shrieks, lunging at us in such a menacing way we back up.

"He said he wouldn't take my recipe for free. For free! Then he said second place is for losers! How dare he talk to me like that! I grabbed the nearest knife just to frighten him. I thought if I waved it around, he'd get scared and beg me not to hurt him. I wanted to listen to him beg like he listened to me try to persuade him to buy my recipe. But instead of begging, he lunged at me. Hard! What was I supposed to do? Drop the knife? Of course not! So you see, in a way, it's like I killed him in self-defense, right?"

"But after killing him in so-called self-defense, you drove out to the enchanted orchard and dumped him in a hole," Wendy points out.

"I was sure no one would believe me." Lillian pouts.

"Is that when you decided to frame the Whitmans?"

"Yes, we know all about it," Juliet says when Lillian's jaw drops in shock.

"I planned to frame Evelyn, assuming she'd be in the bakery like she always was at that time. But when I got to the bakery after, uh, dealing with Bellamy, they were in there talking! It was after midnight, and they were still there. I mean, who does that? Ugh! I was so annoyed. I had to wait around forever and I don't mind telling you it was so inconvenient. But they finally left. That's when I broke in, and tossed one of my knives onto a shelf. I assure you, I wasn't happy about throwing away one of my good knives either. Then I left a drop of blood on an apron and got myself out of there!" She shakes her head pausing to revel in her own brilliance.

"But I didn't realize Evelyn was going to hold some stupid noon press conference, leaving Harold in the bakery instead. I assumed she was going to whine about how she'd been wrongly accused of murder and she was sure it was all a mistake and blah blah blah. I was so sure that would be it. The town would finally turn on her. Then I would win first place in the peach cobbler contest!" She claps her hands with glee.

"So, imagine my surprise when she admitted her family stole the recipe instead! That wasn't part of my plan. I hate it when Evelyn messes with my plans... Hey, do you think they'll make her give back the awards since it wasn't really her recipe? Will she get an asterisk next to her name instead? What if they give me the awards?" she suggests, looking hopeful.

"I thought we'd have to force a confession out of her," Juliet whispers. "I didn't expect her to go on like this."

"Do you think it's the stress of the shifters?" I whisper back.

"Beats me!" Juliet shrugs.

"By the way," I ask Wendy quietly, as the police begin arriving in droves, "how did you know the police were on their way?"

"I didn't. I just guessed," she giggles.

After the police arrive, there's a flurry of activity to take Lillian into custody and search the scene.

Once we've given them our statements we head back to the VW and I turn to Wendy. "Where's the peach blossom? Did you put it back in your pocket?"

"I think I dropped it," she says, looking stricken.

"You dropped it? You have a magic peach blossom and you drop it?"

"One minute it was there, the next it was gone."

"Did you drop it, or did it disappear?" Juliet asks.

"We have to go back and look for it!" I tell them.

"But the cops are all over the place now, they'll never let us back in there to look for a peach blossom. Enchanted or otherwise."

"That's a bummer. Do you think we'll ever find one again?" I ask.

"Call me crazy, but I kind of hope not," she responds.

"Yeah, I get it. This vacation turned out to be more work than I planned. It will be nice to get home and rest."

When we return to the bus, Mystery asks, "Did we miss anything good?"

"Are you all right? When I saw the police, I got worried," Clara says.

"I don't even know where to start," I tell them.

We drive to the inn in complete silence. The police at the scene assured us all charges against Harold were being dropped and he would be released shortly. The security camera on the store across the street recorded the Whitmans inside the bakery at 11 PM, just like they said. It also recorded them leaving around 1 AM and Lillian sneaking in shortly after.

"So, we did all this for nothing?" Wendy whines.

"We watched the peach orchard get saved," I point out.

When we pull up in front of the Peach Blossom Inn & Retreat, Genevieve is waiting for us.

"Are you okay? I was getting worried," she says.

After we explain to her what happened, she's tells us she isn't surprised.

"But Jasper told me that the Indigo Midnight Shifters thrive on chaos and mischief and like to cause trouble. This group was anything *but* trouble," I tell her.

"I have to believe they knew their world was being threatened. It's one thing for them to play practical jokes on people during a normal blue moon, but entirely another when their beloved peach orchards are at stake. I suspect that's what made them act together for the good of the town. But don't you worry, the next true blue moon is three years from now in May. I'm sure they'll be extra mischevious then to make up for it."

"Three years? Wow! So we got to see something extraordinary."

"Yes, you did," Genevieve smiles knowingly.

"You'll never believe this, but Wendy says she lost the enchanted blossom!"

"Oh my dear, she didn't lose it. It will appear again to another needy individual during the next blue moon. Now, now, it's been a long weekend for you," she says, hugging each of us. "You must be exhausted. Agnes has prepared a special dinner for you as a thank you for saving our town."

"Oh, thank goodness, I'm starving!" Wendy exclaims.

Chapter 19

"Do we have enough peaches?" I ask, pulling onto I-70 to return home after our so-called vacation.

"Several cases!" Juliet exclaims.

"I canned peaches with my mother when I was a little girl," Clara says thoughtfully. "We canned all sorts of things, corn, beans, cherries, pretty much everything we grew in the garden. She stored them in the cellar."

"Did you make peach jam?" I ask.

"Oh my, yes!"

"Can you teach me how to make it?"

"I would be delighted!" Clara cheers.

"Will you use your peaches in the bakery?" I ask Juliet.

"Heck no! These are all for me!" she laughs. "But don't tell anyone I said it."

"Next time we go on a vacation, wouldn't it be nice to have an actual vacation?" Wendy proposes. "Or would we be bored?" she muses.

"We met some interesting people this weekend!" Juliet points out.

"Mystery and I met many fascinating ghosts in Palisade. They were so happy to have new ghosts to talk to," Clara says.

"So you weren't bored, stuck in the bus the entire time? I worried you'd long to be home in front of the TV."

"Not at all. My dear, you didn't tell me what Evelyn plans to do with the recipe now."

"From now on it will be known as the Miller-Whitman family recipe," I explain.

"How did the town react after they had a chance to process the news?"

"They've known Evelyn for so long and are so in love with her peach cobbler they didn't care she inadvertently lied about it. They only want more cobbler."

"I hope the judge isn't too harsh on Harold for filing a false report with the police," Wendy says.

"Considering he's never had so much as a parking ticket, the lawyer is certain they'll only give him community service. And perhaps a small fine."

"Hey, have you discovered who's causing trouble at the radio station yet?" Wendy asks.

"Not yet. But it's at the top of my list. Now that vacation is over."

"Ohhh, I know what we should do next! A ski vacation!"

"Where?" Juliet asks. "Skiing is dangerous."

Thank goodness Regular Juliet is back. Vacation Juliet was beginning to worry me.

"How about Vail?" Wendy proposes, ignoring Juliet's warning as usual.

"We could stay in Glenwood and ski," I point out.

"Orrr go to Vail!" Wendy continues.

"We'll see. I think I've sworn off vacations for the time being."

"But it would be so much fun. It's breathtaking at Christmas," she presses.

"I said we'll see," I groan. "You're as bad as Mystery and Clara trying to talk me into things!"

(Peach Cobbler Recipe on the next page!)

Chapter 20
Peach Cobbler Recipe

6 large ripe peaches, pitted, and sliced (I used a combination of strawberries and peaches. You could add any berries you'd like.)

1 cup all-purpose flour (I needed 1 1/4 cups flour – my advice is start with 1 cup and if you need more, add it)

3/4 cup granulated sugar (1/4 is mixed with fruit in the beginning and 1/2 is added to dry ingredients)

1 teaspoon baking powder

1/2 teaspoon ground Saigon cinnamon (you don't have to use Saigon cinnamon – I just like it)

1/2 teaspoon ground ginger

1/2 teaspoon ground nutmeg

1/4 teaspoon salt

1/2 cup unsalted melted butter (plant based worked for me)

1/2 cup milk (creamy oat milk worked for me)

1 teaspoon vanilla extract

Topping:

1/4 cup granulated sugar

1/2 teaspoon ground Saigon cinnamon

Instructions:

Preheat oven (or grill!) to 375 degrees, grease a 9x9 baking dish

In a large mixing bowl, combine sliced peaches with 1/4 cup sugar. Stir well to coat.

In a separate bowl whisk together flour, remaining 1/2 cup sugar, baking powder, cinnamon, ginger, and nutmeg, and salt.

Add melted butter, milk, and vanilla extract to the dry ingredients. Stir until just combined. Batter should be thick.

Pour batter into the baking dish, spread evenly.

Arrange peaches evenly on top of the batter.

In a small bowl, combine 1/4 cup sugar, and cinnamon. Sprinkle mixture over peaches.

Bake 40-45 minutes or until peaches are bubbling and topping is golden brown.

More Books by B I Skinner

Ghostly Glenwood Mysteries Paranormal Cozy Mysteries

The Case of the Haunted Hotel

The Case of the Pilfering Poltergeist

The Case of the Poached Peridot

The Case of the Gym Ghost

The Peach Cobbler Caper

The Case of the Haunted Radio Station (pre-order)

Spooky Shanty Realty Mysteries

Afterlife in the Attic(Pre-order)

Marcall's Breakfast Cafe Paranormal Cozy Mysteries

An Eggscellent Day for Murder

24 Carrot Caper

Daggers and Donuts

Cupcakes and Corpses

A Crime of Cranberry

Peppermints & Pandemonium

Star Spangled Homicide

Blood Curdling Ballots

Sign up for my email list here

https://mailchi.mp/9ebce0da866a/email-signup-list

Visit my website

biskinnerauthor.com

Follow me on Instagram **@bethiskinner** Facebook **@biskinnerauthor**

www.ingramcontent.com/pod-product-compliance
Lightning Source LLC
Chambersburg PA
CBHW051835130726
47987CB00002B/554